THE
BOOK
OF
WONDERS

JULIEN SANDREL

Translated from the French by
Ros Schwartz

Quercus

First published in the French language as *La chambre des merveilles*
by Éditions Calmann-Lévy, Paris, in 2018

First published in Great Britain in 2019 by Quercus

This paperback edition published in 2020 by

Quercus Editions Ltd
Carmelite House
50 Victoria Embankment
London EC4Y 0DZ

An Hachette UK company

La chambre des merveilles by Julien Sandrel
© Editions Calmann-Lévy, 2018
English translation copyright © 2019 by Ros Schwartz

A CIP catalogue record for this book is available
from the British Library

PB ISBN 978 1 78747 374 4
EB ISBN 978 1 78747 372 0

10 9 8 7 6 5 4 3 2 1

Typeset by Jouve (UK), Milton Keynes

Printed and bound in Great Britain by Clays Ltd, Elcograf S.p.A

Papers used by Quercus are from well-managed forests and
other responsible sources.

Julien Sandrel was born in 1980 in the South of France, and lives in Paris. His first novel, *The Book of Wonders*, was first published in France by Éditions Calmann-Lévy in March 2018. It has become a worldwide phenomenon, selling in more than twenty-five countries and is currently being adapted for film.

Ros Schwartz has translated some ninety works of fiction and non-fiction from French, including a new translation of Antoine de Saint-Exupéry's *The Little Prince* and, most recently, Mireille Gansel's *Translation as Transhumance*. She was made a Chevalier de l'Ordre des Arts et des Lettres in 2009.

For Mathilde
For my daughter and son

So, tell me something, Miss Thelma.
How is it you ain't got any kids?
I mean God gets you something special,
I think you oughta pass it on.

Thelma & Louise, Callie Khouri (writer)

1
My King

1

10:32

'Louis, time to wake up! Come on, I'm not going to say it again: please, get yourself up and dressed, or we'll be late. It's already nine twenty.'

This was the start of what was to become the worst day of my entire life. I didn't know it yet, but there would be a 'before' and an 'after' that Saturday, 7 January 2017. There would forever be 'before' – the minute preceding 10:32 a.m. – with its smiles, fleeting joys and memories imprinted on my brain, which I wish I could freeze for eternity. There would forever be 'after': the *whys*, the *if onlys*, the tears, the screams, the prohibitively expensive mascara running down my cheeks, the wailing sirens, the eyes full of sickening compassion, the gut-wrenching spasm of denial. At the time, of course, I was oblivious to all that. It was a secret that only the gods – if they existed, which I strongly doubted – could know. What were they saying to one another, those divinities, at 9:20? *One more, one less, what difference does it make? Are you sure you know what you're doing? Not really, but why not? You're right – why not? – it won't change the world.* I was far from all that, far from the gods, far from my heart. At that moment, I was just me, so close to the tipping point, the moment of rupture, of no return. I was just me, and I was furious at Louis, who was making no effort whatsoever.

My son was driving me up the wall. I'd been trying to coax him out of bed for half an hour, with no success. We were meeting my mother at midday for brunch – a monthly ordeal – and I'd planned to dash over to Boulevard Haussmann beforehand to buy myself the pair of blood-red heels I'd been lusting after since the start of the sales. I wanted to wear them on Monday, for the meeting with the head of Hégémonie, the cosmetics group I'd been working for, night and day, for some fifteen years. I managed a team of twenty people, dedicated to the noble cause of innovation and advertising for a shampoo brand that eliminated up to a hundred per cent of dandruff – the 'up to' meant that one tester out of the two hundred in the trial had seen her tresses entirely rid of flakes. My great triumph had been to obtain authorization to make that claim, after a series of bitter battles with Hégémonie's legal department. Crucial for sales, for my annual pay rise, my summer holiday with Louis – and for my new shoes.

Louis made a few groaning noises before deciding to cooperate. He pulled on a pair of skinny jeans with a too-low waist, splashed some water on his face, spent five minutes skilfully mussing up his hair, refused to wear a hat despite the freezing temperature outside, mumbled a few incomprehensible phrases I knew by heart ('But why do I have to come with you?'), put on his shades, grabbed his skateboard – a dirty board, covered in tags, for which I had to buy competition wheels every five minutes – put on his red, ultra-light Uniqlo puffa jacket, grabbed a packet of chocolate biscuits while guzzling a Frube, just like when he was five, and finally pressed the lift button. I glanced at my watch. 10:21. Perfect; I'd still be able to carry out my precision-timed plan. I had factored in an extra hour, the ritual of getting my Sun King Louis out of bed being completely unpredictable.

It was a glorious day, a cloudless blue winter sky. I've always loved cold light and I have never seen a bluer, purer sky than when I was on a business trip to Moscow. For me, the Russian capital is the queen of winter skies. Paris, that morning, had a Muscovite feel and lay winking in the sun. Once out of our apartment, in the tenth arrondissement, Louis and I made our way along the Saint-Martin canal towards the Gare de l'Est, weaving in and out of families out for a stroll and tourists mesmerized by the sight of a barge going through the Pont Eugène-Varlin lock. I watched Louis race ahead on his skateboard and felt a surge of pride at the little man he was becoming. I should have told him – that sort of thought is meant to be spoken aloud, otherwise it's useless – but I didn't. Louis had changed a lot, in recent months. A growth spurt typical of his age had seen him morph from a puny little boy into a sturdy adolescent, with facial hair starting to show on his still-chubby cheeks, but no spots yet. A fine-looking young man in the making.

Life was all going too fast. I pictured myself for a moment, ambling down Quai de Valmy, my right hand steering a petrol-blue buggy, my left clutching my mobile phone. I do believe that image made me smile a fraction. Or did I dream it up, in hindsight? My memory plays tricks on me; it's so hard to remember my thoughts during those all-important seconds. If only I could turn the clock back a few minutes, I'd be more attentive. If only I could turn it back a few months, a few years, I'd change so many things.

I heard the latest song by The Weeknd – the ringtone Louis had installed on my smartphone. It was JP. Shit. Why was my boss calling me on a Saturday morning? Of course, it had happened before; you can't work for a company like Hégémonie without having to deal with the occasional emergency. Whenever I think about it now, whenever I hear someone say 'emergency', the word has a whole different meaning. Never again will I use the word to talk about a presentation that needs wrapping up, a consumer trial that has to be launched, a bottle design that has to be approved. What kind of emergency is that, exactly? Whose life is in the balance? But, at that precise moment, I didn't see things that way. I simply wondered what emergency JP could need to discuss with me, and I had a feeling it was to do with Monday's meeting. So, a major emergency. Vital. I answered without hesitation, barely noticing that Louis had slowed down and was standing beside me, visibly wanting to say something. I signalled to him that I was on the phone, couldn't he see that? He mumbled into his nascent beard, muttering that it was important, I think. I gestured it was an urgent call, and now I'll never know what he wanted to talk to me about. I'm certain that my parting thoughts before Louis sped off were negative ones. Something to do with his constant need for attention, my never having a moment to myself, his teenage selfishness, my need for a bit of space. Shit. I think the last word that formed in my mind on the subject of my little person – the baby I rocked for hours on end, the baby I sang to for hours on end, who had brought me so much laughter, pride and joy – the last word I mentally uttered in my rusty brain cells was a swear word. How shocking. What a grim memory.

Louis heaved an exaggerated sigh, grabbed the red headphones that had been looped around his neck, rammed them on to his head, yelled something about it always being the same with me, how I only cared about my job, then he pushed off with his right foot and launched the skateboard down the sloping pavement. If I hadn't been talking to JP – the emergency was a problem with some PowerPoint slides that needed redoing – I'd have had a maternal reflex and yelled, *Slow down – you're going too fast*, which annoys any child over kindergarten age, the sort of reprimand that's useless, in theory, but which, in practice, can always stir a half-sleeping conscience. The cry remained unuttered. Having kids is frowned on at Hégémonie, even if the official policy is clear: Hégémonie is pro gender equality; Hégémonie invests in the careers of women in the company. There's always a gulf between theory, stated policy, and practice, that other face of the same company, those unsaid things that result in a ridiculously low number of women on the boards of large corporates. I'd always fought to get to the top, so it was out of the question to display the slightest maternal streak in the midst of a work conversation, even on a Saturday, even at 10:31.

While JP was telling me about the changes that needed to be made by Sunday evening, I kept half an eye on Louis, who was definitely going too fast. I noticed the headphones glued to his ears, and I distinctly remember hoping he hadn't turned the volume up too loud, and that he was aware how fast he was going. I shook my head, telling myself he was a big boy now,

8

that I had to stop worrying about every little thing, about everything, about nothing – especially about nothing. It's incredible all the thoughts that occur in the space of a few seconds. It's incredible how a few seconds can become so painfully etched in your mind.

Last glance at my smartphone screen. It's 10:32. I tell myself I must put the phone down on JP in three minutes max, because we're close to the Métro station.

I hear a muffled wail that reminds me of the horn of an ocean liner in distress. It's a lorry. I look up and time stands still. I am a hundred metres away, but the clamour of the onlookers is so loud that I feel as if I'm already on the spot. My phone smashes on the ground. I howl. My ankle twists, I fall over, get up, remove my stilettos and run as I've never run before. The lorry has stopped now. I'm not the only one screaming. A dozen people who were sitting at a café terrace in the sunshine on this beautiful winter's morning have jumped to their feet. A father covers his son's eyes. How old is he? Four or five, probably. This kind of scene is not for him. Even in films, this kind of scene is never shown. To anyone. At most, it can be suggested. I get closer and scream again. I fling myself to the ground, grazing my knees, but I don't feel the pain. Not that pain, in any case. Louis. Louis. Louis. Louis. My love. My life. How can I describe the indescribable? A witness, later, used the word *she-wolf*. The cries of a she-wolf being disembowelled. I fight, I claw the

9

ground, my body's shaking, I cradle Louis's head in my hands. I know I mustn't touch him, that he mustn't be moved, but I can't . . . Always that same gap between theory and reality. I can't leave him lying on the ground and do nothing. Yet I cradle his head and do nothing other than wait, crying, constantly checking his breathing. Is he breathing? He's breathing. He's stopped breathing. He's breathing again. The emergency services arrive in record time. A fireman takes charge of me, or rather he tries to pull me off Louis. I slap him. I apologize. He smiles at me. I remember everything: his gestures that are both firm and gentle, his unsightly nose, his comforting voice, his formulaic words, the ambulance driving off. I catch a few snatches. Paediatric A & E. Robert Debré Hospital. Intensive care. 'Everything will be all right, madame.' No, it won't be all right. 'I'll drive you there.' I crumple. He holds me. My muscles, tensed up since the accident, have just given way. Someone sits me on a chair on the sun-drenched terrace of the café. My body no longer responds. My stomach is in knots; I throw up my breakfast all over the table of the hipster bar, which empties within seconds. I wipe my mouth, drink a glass of water and look up.

Nothing has changed around me. The sky is still as blue and pure. I look at my watch – also smashed; the face cracked, hands stopped. A motionless witness. It is still 10:32.

One morning

My name's Louis. I live in Paris and I'm twelve and a half, nearly thirteen. I love soccer, manga, the rapper Maître Gims, Pokémon YouTube channels, Nutella, films from the Nineties and 2000s (no, that's not uncool), the smell of exhaust fumes, funky skateboards, Madame Ernest, my maths teacher's boobs, maths without Madame Ernest's boobs, my super Granny Odette, my mother (most days).

Apart from that, I think I'm dead.

I don't normally like talking about myself, but, given the situation and since you're there, I may as well tell you a bit about who you're dealing with and what happened.

I live with just my mum. Her name's Thelma. I spent my last morning with her. I wish I could tell you that it was a wonderful morning, that we shared some magic moments, that we hugged affectionately and said loving words to each other. Actually, it was a horribly ordinary morning, which isn't really surprising. We don't live every hour of every day as if it was our last, that would be exhausting. We just live, that's all. And that's exactly what my life with my mother was like.

So, when I think back, that morning was perfect. I know that Mum must feel very differently about it, I know she must be going over every detail of those last minutes in her mind and wondering what she should have done, what she could have changed. I have the answer, although I know Mum would disagree: nothing.

That's a weird thing to say when you know that our morning together boils down to Mum trying to get me out of bed, me complaining, dilly-dallying and complaining some more. That's how it looked from the outside. That's also what I saw. Now that I've got some (a lot of) distance, I'm conscious of my sensations – of that vague feeling, those tingles in the brain that only become accessible when there's nothing else. The burden of habit. The joy of habits. The unchanging pleasure of family rituals. Those little day-to-day gestures that define us and that change everything.

That morning was filled with those ritual pleasures. The squeak of my bedroom door-handle stirring a tiny fraction of my consciousness, heralding the arrival of the coming day. Mum entering my room, walking over and running her hand through my hair, stroking me from my forehead to the back of my neck – never the other way around. Mum whispering, 'Good morning, Louis, darling. It's time to get up, sweetheart,' as if I were still two or three years old. That moment, hovering between sleep and waking, that lethargic state in which dream and reality are blurred. Then the sound of the electric shutter being rolled up, the sun's rays striking my face, a groan, I turn over and bury my head under the pillow. Mum goes out. Sleep enfolds me once more; I pick up the thread of a dream, of which I'll have no recollection. Mum comes back in, her voice more insistent, not so soft, firmer. Like every day. She knows this ritual inside out too. The same for years. Even if it's become a reflex, we both recognize what the mood of the day will be like from the tone of a syllable uttered, the length of a guttural sound emanating from the sleepy adolescent bear. The mood of the day is happy. It's Saturday, we know it. We have plenty of time, even if Mum says we don't. I know the plan for the day, I know Mum, I know she wakes me up early to give me time to surface.

I'll digress, here, because I know you're saying to yourself, It's strange, this twelve-and-a-half-year-old kid using all those big words, isn't it? At any rate, I can tell you my mates in class 8C of Paul Éluard High School think I'm a freak. It's weird being in with fourteen-year-olds at twelve-and-a-half, anyway. I don't make a big deal of it, but that's how it is and that's how I talk and I can't do anything about it, and at school they make fun of my turns of phrase, calling me a geek, so thank you very much, but don't you start . . .

Now, where was I? Oh, yes – I was telling you. For the past few days, I wanted – I needed – to talk to Mum about this girl I met at football – yup, there are girls who play football, and, yup, they can be pretty. Enough stereotyping. I was waiting for the right moment. Mum and I are shy about our feelings. Not the sort to wear our heart on our sleeve. We tend to keep things

13

to ourselves. The right moment to talk to my mother is not on a weekday. She comes home from work exhausted and finds it hard to switch off her smartphone, always dealing with what she calls 'emergencies'. I wonder what kind of emergency you have to cope with when you're in charge of anti-dandruff shampoo.

Whatever. I said to myself that this ordinary morning on an ordinary weekend was the perfect time. I didn't want Mum to get too carried away and imagine me already married, so I didn't intend to make a big deal of it. An informal chat, casual, was all I wanted. So, when I went up to her and Mum brushed me away like a bramble on her path, I must say, I was fuming. Mum says I'm a bit hot-headed. I'm not too sure what that means – probably that I'm a pain. Or touchy. Or both. In my defence, as Granny Odette says, the apple never falls far from the tree, and Mum is especially touchy. I didn't say she was a pain – you jumped to that conclusion, admit it.

So I snorted like a bull and shot off. I wanted to mess up her work call. It was Saturday morning; somehow, I had to get her to realize that it wasn't a work day. I'm very aware that Mum stresses when she sees me vanish around a street corner. Consciously or not, she starts walking faster so as not to lose sight of me. So I shot off, I wanted to pass the corner of Rue des Récollets before her, then hide inside the entrance to Jardin Villemin, give her a bit of a scare and make her end her call.

I'm not quite sure what happened next. Well, yes, I think I understand; I'm not dumb. I was going too fast, for sure. I lost control. A really stupid mistake. I never lose control like that; I can handle my board. I looked up and saw the lorry coming. I heard the sound of a horn, then everything went black.

Total blackout.

Contrary to popular belief, I didn't see my life flash by in a few tenths of a second, I just saw the headlights of that rotten lorry and I thought, Hey, that's weird he's got his headlights on in broad daylight.

Last thoughts are surprisingly mundane.

2

E.E.G.

At no point did I think he might be dead. Mothers must be programmed that way. To consider the possibility of your child dying is already to bury them. And burying a child is quite simply impossible. Louis wasn't dead. He couldn't be dead.

I was in shock. I don't know if that's the official, medical term, but I think I heard someone say the word. I experienced the rest of that arctic Saturday floating in a haze, as if sounds and sensations were deadened by a cocoon enveloping me from head to toe. I felt anaesthetized – perhaps thanks to the tranquillizers that I was immediately given, perhaps as a result of the bombshells that were being dropped around me, one after the other.

Emotional bombshells, like when the doctors explained to me that they had pumped my son full of drugs to prevent him from suffering, that the priority was to stop any infections that would cause internal lesions. That his condition was life-threatening, that for the time being it was impossible to assess his real state of consciousness because of the medication, that they would have to wait until the treatment was finished to have a clearer idea. 'We're very sorry, madame.'

Then, tear bombshells when my mother arrived at the hospital, shook me, screaming, blaming my inertia, my irresponsibility, my inattentiveness. The doctors had to drag her away from me – my own mother. 'Everyone reacts to this kind of situation differently, madame; you must respect your daughter's response, as we respect yours; and, no, we're not arrogant little fools.'

And word bombshells. Legions of new words, acronyms, incomprehensible signals, armies of adjectives, little medical soldiers that only make sense if you want to hear them. From this fug, the only ones I remembered were the key words, those markers that you sense play a crucial part and are more important than the others.

Multiple trauma.

Haematomas.

Intracerebral.

Pulmonary.

Coma.

Deep.

Respirator.

E.E.G.

Electroencephalogram.

Wait.

How long?

No idea.

Unpredictable.

Never?

No idea.

Too soon.

Hope.

Courage.

In his hospital bed, Louis was beautiful. Serene. Calm. Surprisingly intact. If it weren't for all those tubes, his face and the rest of his body would have looked unbroken, or almost. Two smashed ribs, a fractured leg – and, since the fracture wasn't open, immobilizing the leg would be sufficient, so I was told. To which I replied that I couldn't see the point of immobilizing the leg, given that Louis wasn't exactly going to be prancing around straight away. The nurse shot me one of those judgemental looks that speak volumes, deeming wisecracks from the mouth of a distraught mother inappropriate. I was a bewildered mother. I don't know about distraught. Everything felt unreal. This is a nightmare, Thelma, that's all. You're going to wake up, and Louis will be beside you, his tousled surfer's locks tumbling over his dark eyes, which will begin to laugh through their thick lashes. *What's up, Mum? Don't you like my pranks any more? OK, that one was a bit off, but I'm fine, don't worry. By the way,*

did you buy me that Pokémon-EX card I found on Amazon?
What are we having for supper tonight? Can I watch the con-
cert on MTV? Go on, pleeaase, Mum, be cool. You're the best.
I love you.

I'm so far from being the best. The best and I are light
years apart. She mocks me from her far-off galaxy. Her
son is standing beside her, smiling. He's alive. And mine?

Alive.

Hope.

Wait.

How long?

No idea.

3

IMMEDIATELY AFTER

I was permitted to leave the hospital on the Sunday
evening. The staff wouldn't let me out on the Saturday;
they needed to keep me under observation – that was
the official line. But I think they were mainly afraid I'd
do something stupid. They don't know me. If there's
one thing I'm not, it's suicidal. I have a deeply ingrained
survival instinct. Even in my darkest moments, I find
the strength to pick myself up again. That's what I'd
been telling myself over and over since Louis's accident.
I was going to have to go into battle mode. And that's
something I know how to do. I'm a warrior. A fighter.
'That's very good, madame; Louis is going to need your
support. The family has an important part to play when
a person's in a coma. There are no guarantees, mind
you, but Louis is very young. At his age, he's more likely
to recover. Positive outcomes in such cases are often
thanks to a combination of specialist medical care, a
young patient who keeps fighting and the support of a
loving family.'

So I left the hospital on the Sunday with hope in my heart, but death in my soul. Outwardly, I wanted to fight with him, and the nurses had boosted my hopes. Especially the adorable fair-haired one who reminded me of the T.V. presenter Sophie Davant, and to whom I could have confided my most private fears in front of the cameras. But, deep down, a sickening voice inside my head – goaded by a night of searching *coma* online (and the Internet is a risky place to look for information about something like that) – kept whispering, *What's the use? A stage-three coma and it's hopeless. Remember Michael Schumacher? He's been in a coma for years. Supposing Louis wakes up with locked-in syndrome? Supposing he never wakes up?* I was veering from total despair to the wildest optimism, causing the hospital staff to fear for my mental state. I wanted to tell them not to worry, that I was always like that but today it was more extreme, but I wasn't sure that would reassure them and I had to get out of there, otherwise I really would go mad.

On Sunday, I was allowed to spend the whole day with Louis. My slumbering child. I expected to see him wake up, turn over and groan that it was much too early for a Sunday. I would have given everything to hear one of those groans of his that ordinarily so annoyed me. But nothing of the sort happened. Nothing happened. The machine regulated his breathing, but his chest was the only part of his body that appeared to be active. I held his hand for most of the day. I massaged his palms, his fingers. His feet too, for ages, slowly. The feel of his warm body comforted me. On his face, I was allowed only to stroke his cheeks. I closed my eyes and saw the little dimple that always appeared when he smiled. I cried, a lot – over his hands, in mine. I sang him lullabies. I hummed his favourite a dozen or so times, the one he still asked for at the age of twelve. The one I'd made up, with my own words. Probably the most tuneless, probably the least pretty lullaby of all. Probably the most beautiful, in his eyes and in mine.

As the sun went down, I felt scared. Most of all, I feared going back to our place alone. To have to face him, without him. To have to open the door, inhale the pungent teenage fragrance he spritzed himself with every morning, pick up the dirty clothes he'd flung into the passage to the utility room, as was his habit. Eat. Sleep. Not sleep. The night before, I'd been given sleeping tablets, and, exhausted, I'd fallen into a dreamless sleep. But this first night without him would be different. I saw it coming and slammed on the brakes, pretending not to hear the nurses who, for the past few minutes, had been gently signalling to me that I'd have to leave soon, that I couldn't stay. And that this was likely to go on. That I'd have to be strong, for him. I gave him a long, drawn-out kiss, whispered things that only he and I would understand. I stood up and walked out of his

room, leaving behind my baby and my previous existence. I was going to have to face up to life 'after'.

I decided to walk home, persuaded that the fresh air
would do me good after breathing the stale, recycled
hospital air. After a few hundred metres in the heavy
traffic of a Parisian Sunday evening, I began to think
about the lorry driver who had turned my life upside
down. Police officers had come to talk to me, but I was
in such a state that the doctors had told them to leave
me in peace. But they'd replied that I was going to have
to give a statement. They came back later, and I talked
to them for around ten minutes. I had to describe what
I'd seen of the collision, which was not a lot. But I
wanted justice to be done and I began to focus my thirst
for revenge on the lorry driver. The officers were under-
standing and tempered my outbursts demanding life
imprisonment, assuring me that the investigation was
under way, that a number of witnesses had been able to
describe the scene precisely, that it had been recorded
by the C.C.T.V. cameras and they had the film, and that
of course justice would be done. All the same, one of
them had quietly said that it had been an accident, that
I should know that the driver was a woman, a mother
of two young children, and that she too was devastated,
in shock, and that I might not like the findings of the
investigation. All the witness statements concurred: it
seemed fairly clear that Louis had lost control of his

skateboard, and that, despite the driver's best efforts, she had not been able to avoid him. The driver's liability would probably prove negligible. Then I began to rant against the incompetence of the police, screaming that it couldn't have happened as they said, that my son hadn't in any way been at fault in all this, that the driver was a manipulative bitch if she'd got them to believe that she wasn't to blame, that they themselves, those two policemen, were complete idiots, and other expletives that it's difficult for me to transcribe in hindsight. When I leapt up, brandishing an angry fist at them, Sophie Davant and a nursing assistant had come into the room and restrained me, then I crumpled into the arms of the TV-presenter lookalike and on to the cold, green lino floor, racked with frantic sobs. The officers had said that they'd forget my behaviour and what I'd said, wished me strength, and left. I had not only lost my son's future, I'd also lost my dignity. I'd learned that the lorry driver was a woman, a mother too, and I'd wished the worst on her, even though I knew nothing of her life.

I shook my head as I carried on walking towards the Saint-Martin canal. Another fifteen minutes and I'd be home. Our home. Alone.

Soon, my old reflexes kicked in. I glanced at my watch. Face still broken – 10:32. No joy to be expected there. I thrust my right hand into my bag in search of my phone, which I hadn't thought about since the previous day, something that hadn't happened since . . . After rummaging around in my crammed handbag, I realized that my smartphone wasn't in there, and I remembered dropping it at the time of the accident.

I stopped walking. JP. I'd been in the middle of a call from JP. I hadn't got back to him, hadn't spared a single thought for him, for our sodding presentation to Mr Head Honcho, taking place tomorrow. I was supposed to work on the slides on Sunday, and Sunday was today. JP must be in a panic not to have heard a peep from me. A panic over the presentation, naturally. Didn't give a shit about me. I wondered what he might have heard of the accident. Had he been an audio witness, or had the telephone smashed beforehand? I recalled my sensations of the moment and felt certain that the phone had been smashed immediately. JP hadn't heard anything. That reassured me, in a way, because I had no wish to face the contrived sympathetic looks of my colleagues at Hégémonie. My career was going to be my lifeline. If I lost my job, then I would no longer be anyone. I had to cling to that vestige of normality at all costs. Cling on to Thelma the marketing director of the specialty-shampoos division, and not allow her to be buried under Thelma the mother of a child in a coma.

No matter how hard I tried to think about JP and my work, images of the accident continued to haunt me. I heard my own screams echo, felt a rising wave of nausea and couldn't stop myself from vomiting right there, in the middle of the street. I coughed and gagged several times. An old lady, taking her dog for a walk, crossed the road to avoid me. The legendary Parisian concern for others.

I sat on the steps of an apartment building to get my breath back, calm down, distance myself from all the sound and the fury. How long did I sit there like that? Long enough to let my hands, my ears and my cheeks forget the biting cold.

Then, a few thoughts began to take shape. I slowly outlined my new short-term goals. I can't move forward if I don't have goals. I've never lived any other way. Since the accident, all my goals had become irrelevant. So I drew up a new brief but hard-hitting list that would be the focus of all my efforts, all my energy, in the coming days. Afterwards, we'd see.

Goal number one: get Louis out of the coma.

Goal number two: carry on with my job, as before.

That night, which I'd been so dreading, I managed to drop off for an hour or so. The rest of the time, I worked on the presentation. When I'm on my computer, I go into a kind of trance and am oblivious to everything around me.

That was exactly what I needed. Numb my mind by working flat out so as to avoid thinking about Louis.

4

O CAPTAIN! MY CAPTAIN!

'For fuck's sake, Thelma, what the hell were you up to? I called you fifty times it's totally unprofessional you could at least have called me back, fuck it, the stress you cause me I hope you've made all the changes to the presentation otherwise we're in for a bollocking and don't you think I'm going to back you up, baby.'

A breath. The first.

'Love you too, JP. Hello, by the way.'

'Go on, take the piss. Don't you feel bad. For fuck's sake. Lucky I worship you and would do anything for you.'

The guy always says everything and its opposite in the same breath. It drives me insane. All the kids at the office come out of meetings with him completely freaked out, not knowing how to respond to his aggressive injunctions. Having read up on the subject, I'm convinced that JP is a narcissistic pervert. The sort to confuse his victims with his convoluted demands and congratulate them for completing a task while pointing out to them what total losers they are.

'Here, this is the final version of the presentation,' I said, handing him a USB stick.

'I didn't get a wink of sleep last night because of you. You're paid enough not to go AWOL at the weekend when we're seeing the big boss on the Monday. Is that clear?'

'Crystal clear, JP. I won't do it again. Promise.'

Simpering, sidelong glances, the ploys of a little girl, both apologetic and proud – nothing more effective than beating a pervert at his own game and confounding him with attitudes that are in total contradiction to the tone of the words.

JP whizzed through the presentation and gave me a huge smile. I'd done a good job, I knew it. He had no criticisms.

'Well done, miss. You're a pain, but you're good. When I say "good", I mean your skills, of course. Between you and me, you're past your sell-by date, as far as I'm concerned, ha ha. I'm joking, you know I fancy you, you're the prettiest MILF I know. Right, enough messing around, the boss is waiting. Get your knickers off, we're going to have some fun, ha ha.'

Don't worry, JP, I'm not angry with you, it's just that, for the past two years, I've recorded on my iPhone all the charming little utterances that you and your fellow managers have made about me and other women. I wasn't born yesterday.

JP and I took the lift up to the eighth floor. Everyone we passed gratified us with a perfunctory 'Good luck'. Mr Head Honcho was feared by everyone within the company and was a legend outside it. 'An iron fist in an iron glove,' said his fellow C.E.O.s of blue-chip companies. 'A stupid arsehole,' said Hégémonie's Polish workers, whose factories had been shut down recently. A big boss, completely unknown to the general public, but a demigod in the financial world, who must be venerated and, most importantly, never contradicted, at the risk of incurring the wrath of this modern-day dictator.

I have never been afraid of him, doubtless thanks to my upbringing. My mother always used to tell me that, if someone intimidated me, I should imagine them with their trousers down, to humanize them. *Whoever they are, however arrogant or powerful, imagining them on the toilet should reduce them to their rightful place in your mind, my girl: he's a man like any other, who has the same vital needs, but also the same rights and the same obligations as everyone else. Don't ever forget that.*

Ten minutes later, we walked into the meeting room. Thirty or so people were sitting around the table, looking earnest. We're talking cosmetics, after all, which is a very serious subject. In this sort of meeting, there's a bunch of dummies who pretend to be listening, but sit there checking their emails on their laptops, or shopping online. They never say a word, but always agree with the big boss, nodding every time he opens his mouth. When a woman is doing the presentation, she's expected to wear a short skirt and high heels, to be made up with all the company's products: Billion Lashes mascara, Ultra-red lipstick, Vintage Chic eye shadow, New York Fun limited-edition fuchsia nail varnish. At the very least.

Mr Head Honcho likes ridiculing the consumers, whom he condescendingly refers to as the 'little wifeys'; the models in the Hégémonie ads, whom he compares to poultry, demanding we fire them at the first sign of ageing; the factory workers who don't give a fuck, those on the minimum wage, who ought to think themselves lucky to have a job and who could easily be replaced by migrant workers who are happy to live on one euro a day; and the female marketing directors, whose language is peppered with English to disguise the hollowness of their recommendations. Mr Head Honcho's a hoot. And the room's in stitches, of course.

I launch into my presentation and quickly notice that our boss isn't listening. He's tapping on his iPhone with a lewd smile. I can easily imagine the kind of content he's watching. I decide to stop. The damned presentation that I'd worked on all night is for the benefit of him and him alone. If he's not listening, there's no point going on. People clear their throats and glance up at me, wondering what I'm playing at. The rule is that, whatever the attitude of the sovereign, the show must go on.

The C.E.O. looks up at me, my silence having grown deafening, and examines me for a moment. Gobsmacked, he sits up and puts his smartphone down on the table.

'Well, Thelma, sweetheart, what's going on?'

'This presentation is for your benefit, and you're not listening. So I stopped to give you time to deal with your urgent matter.'

'The executive board is here in the room, as well as twenty of the company's most senior managers. This presentation is not only for me, and I don't like your tone. Continue.'

I hesitate. I look at my feet. I must remain unshaken. Take it on the chin, without batting an eyelid. But sod it.

'Which of you gentlemen could sum up the beginning of my presentation?'

Renewed interest among the audience. Sardonic smiles. Frightened looks.

'What are you playing at, Thelma, sweetheart?'

'I am not your sweetheart. Fine. Let's continue.'

I pick up from where I left off, but am conscious that he is plotting something. He interrupts me mid-sentence.

'No, we're not going to continue. Your presentation isn't ready; it's amateurish. Come back and see me when you've reworked it. I thought I knew what kind of woman you were, Thelma, sweetheart, and that pleased me greatly. Do you have any children, Thelma?'

A vision. Incongruous, unexpected in this work environment. Louis. The lorry. The hospital. Quick, banish those images.

'I have a son, sir, but I don't see the connection. What kind of woman am I, in your view? And, at the risk of repeating myself, I am not your sweetheart.'

'You're the sort to put your career before everything else, the sort who'll do anything to climb the ladder, if you get my drift. And that's very good; no one here is complaining.'

Lascivious smile, again. Sniggering around the room. I see myself walking beside the Saint-Martin canal. It's 10:31. Louis is trying to talk to me. I'm on the phone. I put my career before everything else. This man is right. I feel a mounting nausea. And tears. He goes on.

'I have a horror of those women who do fuck all with their time, unless they buy my products, of course. I thought you were different, that you were devoted to this company, body and soul. I was mistaken. Perhaps you should have spent a little less time mothering and a little more time on this presentation. This meeting is over, Thelma, dear.'

He gets up. I feel a blind anger rumbling inside me.

Mothering. I picture myself at Louis's bedside, the previous day. Mothering my damaged teenager. Trying desperately to make myself useful to him. Trying to hide my grief, then abandoning that hopeless pretence. I see myself with Louis on his first day at school. Mothering my little boy. Slipping a bar of his favourite chocolate into his school bag, with a little drawing of a red heart to comfort him and tell him that I'm there, at his side, always. I see myself cradling Louis in the maternity ward. Mothering my baby. Alone. Feeling like a bad mother because I can't breastfeed him properly. My breasts are painful, but I can't do it. Louis loses weight, I'm advised to bottle-feed him, but I persevere. I don't give up. Two days later, Louis begins to feed and I start to cry. Mothering – don't talk to me about mothering.

This bastard has no idea what he's saying. I walk over to him and I do what I should have done a long time ago. What all the women in the company should have done a long time ago. I plant myself in front of the dictator, blocking his path, and I slap him as hard as I can.

A Slap with a capital S.

The ultimate slap.

The super-slap.

The mother of all slaps.

It'll cost me dearly. I'll be fired, I know. But what a buzz! What an amazing feeling. The chief tosser stares at me, speechless. He raises his hand to his cheek, then smiles at me and says, to no one in particular:

'Fire her now!'

I reply, quite simply:

'It'll be a pleasure, sir.'

I leave the room in a state I've never experienced before. I think I'm about to burst into tears. Instead, I burst out laughing.

5

LET MY HEART GIVE UP

I had failed. My second goal was totally screwed. One thing was now certain: I would not be carrying on my career as before. I thought I'd be feeling really bad, but, from the next day, my shoulders were lighter and I was able to spend entire days at Louis's bedside. I told him about my performance, the way I'd put that vile pig of a C.E.O. in his place. I really went to town, acting out the scene, making the nurses laugh – especially Sophie Davant, who whispered confidentially that there was a lot to be done on that front in the hospital too, that the place was full of misogynists and that hearing my story gave fresh hope to all the women, humiliated daily, in that testosterone-fuelled environment. I wanted to tell my mother all about the incident, and, for the first time in years, I reckoned she'd be proud of me. But I quickly stifled that notion. I had no wish to see her rock up in my life; she was persona non grata. I'd given her permission to visit Louis, but had carefully avoided running into her. I decided we'd take turns to sit with him.

Louis was still unresponsive. I wanted to let him know that I wouldn't be defeated, and tried to brighten up his days as much as possible. The doctors had been clear: it was very unlikely that he could hear anything, but there was a tiny chance, so I clung to that and wanted to show him that his mother was fighting, that his mother hadn't given up.

When I got home in the evenings, anxious to wind down, I'd sink into a profound despair. Then I'd allow myself to cry, a glass of red wine in hand, followed by another, and then the entire bottle. I felt better afterwards, drifting in a state of reverie. In my recurrent daydream, Louis manages to stop in time on that damned kerb, and he turns around and begins to laugh, making a skateboarder's signal, meaning, *All good, Mum*. We laugh together and set off again in the direction of the Gare de l'Est, arm in arm. In the morning, in real life, I'd wake up with a hangover, gulp down a couple of paracetamols with my coffee, ignore the phone messages and emails from my mother, and leave for the hospital.

*

Three days after the momentous slap, brandishing my letter of dismissal for serious professional misconduct, I went to see a lawyer and told him what had happened. He pulled a face, implying that I was in big trouble . . .

until I revealed the trump cards I'd been carefully keeping up my sleeve: fifteen years of excellent and loyal service at Hégémonie, glowing appraisals, dozens of clandestine audio recordings of everyday sexism in the company, and – an unhoped-for extra – the spontaneous sympathetic email from one of the few women who had been at that fateful meeting, saying she'd be prepared to testify in my favour, on condition of anonymity.

My lawyer's face brightened. I'd done a good job, my case was cast iron: never would a group like Hégémonie, whose business relied entirely on the trust of women all over the world, run the risk of a sexual-harassment scandal that could cost them a boycott, tens of millions of euros in losses and a major P.R. crisis. He would start negotiations with them that would see me financially secure for many years to come. In his view, I could easily obtain some half a million euros or more, but we could aim higher by putting the frighteners on the great behemoth.

And so the recording of one of the commander-in-chief's favourite jokes was sent to Hégémonie's lawyers. Mic on, the scene begins. The marketing team is presenting a new ad featuring Jennifer Preston-Conwell, triple Oscar winner, with some thirty million social-media followers. Mr Head Honcho unceremoniously interrupts the speaker.

'Your Jennifer's beginning to age. She's costing us a

fortune in photoshopping. She needs liposuction, if you ask me.'

Pause. Palpable embarrassment. Silence. Mr Head Honcho begins to laugh.

'And how can she have such tiny tits and such a fat arse? Inflate her breasts, shave off her arse; it'll be OK for this time, but, after that, find a new muse. Otherwise sales of our body-care products will plummet, and you'll go down with them.'

'Bingo,' crowed my lawyer, his eyes gleaming with mercenary tears.

*

On the ninth day, the medical team decided to halt Louis's treatment. The infections were cured, the bruising reduced. I wanted to believe that Louis was making progress, but the doctors continued to say that his true level of consciousness needed to be assessed now that he was no longer being maintained in an artificial coma. It was now that we would find out whether Louis was showing signs of awareness. How long would it take to know this? In two days' time, we would have a good idea of the situation. Patience. Be brave.

*

I got through that unbearable two-day wait, but I kept bursting into tears at the slightest provocation.

Everything reminded me of Louis. Of his absence. Of missing him. The woman in the bakery said hello, and I welled up at the sight of the macaroons I usually bought for my son. I'd switch on the radio, but couldn't bear all those hip songs that only made the painful silence of my apartment even more poignant. I'd walk in the street and nearly pass out each time I saw a skateboard. I had to sit down on a bench to get my breath back the minute I spotted a lorry. My life was a series of ordeals which I'd never be able to overcome.

My headache grew more searing each day. I'd upped the dose from one bottle of wine to two. The hospital staff weren't blind. They sent their most brilliant representative to see me, in the person of Sophie Davant. They knew she was my favourite, my raw nerve. She talked to me with the utmost gentleness, pushing me to react, giving me the details of a psychiatrist I should go and see without delay; I had a problem; it was pretty standard in my circumstances and it wasn't too late. 'Promise me you'll give him a call.' Yes, I promise, Sophie.

I didn't phone him. I took refuge in silence. I felt wrung out. My lawyer told me that Hégémonie had already raised the bid, that we were close to one million euros. He sounded jubilant, but this news gave me no joy. It was just a piece of information, like any other.

Those few days forced me to open my eyes to the grim reality of my life. Outside my job and my son, I had nothing. I was nothing. My love life was as flimsy as cigarette paper; I hadn't had sex for two whole years.

Even so, I had been all right before. Above average. Slim, five foot six, an intense face with hazel eyes and thick, sensual, well-shaped eyebrows, which I'd always refused to pluck and which emphasized my large eyes. Flaming chestnut hair – that's the adjective my hair stylist used to console me about my unruly mop. I often wore it up, with a pencil stuck through it. I loved the gesture of lifting my thick mass of hair, twisting it and exposing the nape of my neck, letting my skin thrill to the touch – and sometimes enchant, reminding me of my youth.

I'd created a profile on several dating sites, offering my neck, eyebrows and straggly chignon to the eyes of the world. I'd ticked the box saying I was open to one-night stands and had been swamped with offers. Married men, mostly. That had convinced me of the inadequacy of the male sex.

The only real relationship I've ever had was with Louis's biological father. A love affair that lasted nearly two years. But an impossible relationship. He doesn't know he's a father. I've never tried to find out what became of him. Louis has asked me countless times about his dad, my mother has asked me countless times about Louis's father. She's come close to guessing, but I have always refused to say any more. I preferred a simple, exclusive mother–son relationship to an impossible triangle. I chose the broken family rather than the blended-family option.

*

On the evening of the eleventh day, I was called into the family room by the senior consultant. Alexandre Beaugrand was aptly named; he was the hospital heart-throb, with his carefully combed, on-trend haircut and killer smile. In other circumstances, I'd have welcomed a tête-à-tête with him. But his expression was grave. And we were in a room whose decor was too garish. To be honest, I was terrified. I sat down, unable to speak, staring at the floor, my arms folded, biting my lip, fists clenched. Everything inside me had shut down.

Then the doctor explained. Slowly. Choosing his words judiciously. My world fell apart completely. Louis was showing no signs of consciousness. The medical team was very concerned. I'm no longer sure of his exact words. Louis was in what is called a vegetative state. What did that mean, precisely? That he was breathing, that some reflexes were working, that the electroen-cephalograms showed signs of brain activity. Be clear, for fuck's sake! I started to lose my cool. He kept his. He must be used to dealing with parents at breaking point. What he meant was that the graph wasn't flat, so they couldn't declare him brain-dead, but they had observed

43

a sort of anarchic background noise, which meant that Louis's neurons showed a totally illogical activity. His condition was still life-threatening. We were going to have to carry on waiting.

That was when I screamed, I think. Or was it when he said the word I'd been refusing to say to myself for eleven days? Dead. Louis could die. I asked how much longer we'd have to wait until we knew. He was loath to reply. I repeated the question once, and then again, raising my voice each time. My breathing was irregular, I was crying, I ran my hands over my face, through my hair, repeating tirelessly that it wasn't possible. I was going mad. Alexandre Beaugrand kept saying, 'I'm very sorry, madame, I can't answer that.' I demanded that he reply, he couldn't leave me like that, he must have an idea of how long it would be until they knew. They would have to monitor the progress of his body and, most importantly, his brain, day by day. Each time there was a new development, they would be able to reassess his condition. Yes, but what if there were no new developments? If nothing happens, after how long will you decide that there's no hope? Answer me, for fuck's sake! Answer me, I beg you, I need to know. I need to find out.

I found out. I sat down. My heart in pieces. Alexandre Beaugrand placed his hand on my shoulder. I wasn't able to cry. One month. In one month, if there was no change in Louis's condition, the doctors would discuss whether they should continue treating him and might come to the conclusion that they should stop keeping my son artificially alive. If, in a month's time, they felt there was no hope of neurological recovery, they would decide not to subject him to further suffering, not to pursue an unreasonable and unjustifiable course. Then they would turn off the machines. One month. One long month. One tiny month. But we weren't at that point yet. Be brave. Patience. I thanked him, and he asked me once again if I'd be all right, and I replied, 'Yes, of course.'

*

I left the hospital in a daze. I distinctly heard a whistle recognizable among hundreds. A cowboy whistle, the dry whistle of the shepherd calling his dogs, a whistle that I've always loathed. I turned around and saw her standing there, one fist on her hip, her expression hard. My mother. That was the last thing I needed. Not tonight. Especially not tonight.

I pretended not to see her and walked faster. She whistled a dozen more times, as if I were a common dog. I hailed a taxi with tinted windows and dived in. I saw her running towards me, gesticulating madly (my mother's just turned sixty and is fighting fit). I didn't know where to go, but I didn't want to go home. I gave the driver the address of a restaurant. On the spur of the moment, I'd decided to celebrate my son's final month at a Michelin-starred eatery. I'll gloss over that evening, during which, for the first time in my life, a waiter refused to serve me. When I ordered my third bottle of exorbitantly priced wine, I was politely asked to pay my bill and leave. I took it very badly. My memories are a bit hazy, but I think I had to be escorted off the premises and ended up having the meal for free – get that inebriated woman out of here without trying to make her pay, rather than cause a scandal in those hushed surroundings.

I had trouble finding a taxi to take me home. Several stopped but said no when they saw the state I was in. A knight in shining armour, answering to the name of Mamadou, drove me home and deposited me in front of the entrance to my building.

'Are you sure you're all right, madame?'

'Of course, everything's fine, Mr Taxi-Driver.'

The car moved off and I passed out in the double-door entrance before I could enter the code on the internal keypad.

6

30 Days

FIGHT BACK

I woke up in my bed. My head felt as if it was about to explode and I wanted both to throw up and to crawl into a mouse hole, as the memories of the previous evening gradually flooded back. I was mortified. I hoped none of my neighbours had seen me, and I quickly realized that I didn't have the faintest idea how I'd got up to my apartment. My adventure – as far as I knew, but everything was hazy, I had to admit – had ended in the entrance to my building. I got up slowly. I felt giddy. I managed to take a few steps to extricate myself from my bedroom and go into the sitting room.

Whistle – a start, turn around. My mother.

A cook's apron around her waist, a vacuum-cleaner handle in her right hand, her left hand on her hip – her signature stance and sign of her impatience.

'The state you're in, my girl – you look a fright.'

'Good morning, Mother. What are you doing here?'

'I'm having great fun, as you can see. I'm doing a bit of tidying up in this pigsty. I reckoned that you must

47

have let yourself go, but this goes beyond my worst fears. I was on the verge of calling those two girls on the TV who come and clean up the place, in desperate cases.'

I glanced around the room. She was right. I couldn't bring myself to say, *You're right*, which would have choked me, so I said nothing and slumped on the sofa, grabbing a plaid blanket and wrapping it snugly around me.

'Oh, and, by the way, don't look for your plonk; I've chucked it all away.'

'You've what?'

'I've chucked it all away.'

'For fuck's sake, Mum, it's not plonk. You've just thrown away several hundred euros' worth of wine.'

'Watch your language, my girl. Forget the price, look at you. You can't carry on like this. I'm taking things in hand.'

'No, you're not taking things in hand. You're going to leave me alone. If I want to have a little drink from time to time, that's my business, and you're not my cleaner either. Go away, please, Mother.'

'No way. I'm staying.'

'Are you kidding?'

'Do I look as if I'm joking? Do you know what could have happened to you yesterday? You were so drunk that anyone could have taken advantage of you. When that taxi driver dropped you and you passed out, you had your keys on you. If some pervert had come along,

God knows what he could have done to you. I waited for you all evening on the steps. Like a beggar. Luckily, your neighbours recognized me and didn't boot me out. I saw you slumped in the entrance and that was painful. It hurts me to see you like this, Thelma. I've been following you for several days. I'm afraid for you; I'm watching you go downhill, drinking wine by the litre and getting thinner in front of my eyes. I know you're spending your days at the hospital. At first, I thought what you were doing for your son was wonderful, but you're becoming a wreck for all to see. It's not going to help if you slowly kill yourself. If you let yourself go, you won't be able to fight for your son, and, if you can't do it, how is Louis going to find the strength to fight?'

'For fuck's sake, Mum, don't you understand that he's never going to wake up! What do you expect me to fight against? I can fight all right when there's an enemy. But, in this case, there's no one! They've stopped the treatment and nothing's fucking happened! Nothing! Do you know what that means? It means that, if there's no activity in his brain within the next month, they'll stop everything. Thirty days from now, they'll switch off his life support. It'll be over. There'll be nothing. I'm up to my ears in nothingness. Look at me. What do you see? A poor girl who's got nothing left. Who's no longer anything.'

My mother came over to me. She sat on the sofa very

49

close to me and put her hand on my shoulder. That was the first physical contact between us for some ten years, I think. I recoiled, but I left her hand there.

'That's not true. You're wrong. You are much more than you think, but you can't see it any more. You have to get out of this negative spiral. I'm here. Louis is here and the doctors aren't lying. If they're keeping our little man, it's because they're hopeful. You're strong, Thelma. I haven't said so to you for a long time, but I'm proud of you. I'm proud of the woman you've become.'

'Bullshit.'

'For goodness' sake, stop telling me how I feel! You're not inside my head, so let me speak, let me think. I'm moving in with you until further notice.'

I sat up, stung to the quick by a sharp point.

'That is absolutely out of the question.'

'I'm not asking you. I had a set of keys cut while you were asleep.'

I didn't have the energy to fight back. Not right then. I let it go and lay back down on the sofa. My mother stood up and I dozed off, lulled by the hum of the vacuum cleaner. I was thirteen again, and my head hurt so badly . . .

*

That day, for the first time since the accident, I didn't go and visit Louis. I slept all day. When I woke up, my mother was bustling around the kitchen and a familiar aroma was coming from it. A fragrance of the south.

My mother was born in south-east France, and, even though we lived in Paris, we often used to go on holiday to the Riviera, to stay with my Aunt Odile, who died five years ago. Odette and Odile, disastrously named, but a real sisterly pair, those two. Twins. I adored my Aunt Odile, who always concocted tasty little dishes for us. On Bastille Day, in the evening, she always made our favourite, *soupe au pistou*, then we'd go down from the old town of Hyères into the centre to watch the fireworks, the rich flavours of the vegetables and basil still on our tongues. I think I was happy then. I knew very well what my mother was driving at, that evening. I'd recognize the aroma of *soupe au pistou* anywhere. It was a summer dish, and this was 19 January. Too bad. I was starving.

Right away, I noticed how clean the apartment was. My mother had never been particularly fond of housework, and I suspected that she'd brought in Françoise, the woman I employ to do my cleaning, but I didn't say anything. I sat down at the kitchen counter. Two plates, two glasses. I steeled myself for dinner with my mother, just the two of us. A nightmare that would have been unthinkable a few days earlier. Another absurdity in this decidedly topsy-turvy life. My mother smiled at me and asked if I'd slept well. Her turn of phrase, combined with the heady smell of basil, whisked me back thirty years. A sudden whiff of the past. I pictured myself back in the kitchen of our apartment in the Butte-aux-Cailles neighbourhood, a steaming hot chocolate on the table, my mother's smile and her routine question: *Did my little pussycat sleep well?* My mother has always called me her little pussycat. She hadn't uttered those words for ages.

It was a day of firsts. A day of renewal, perhaps.

I lowered my guard and merely replied, 'Yes, thank you, Mum.'

Breaking News

OK, so I'm really sorry because I misled you. I think I'm alive. A bit of a mess, but alive. If we were on the news, a red ticker would say, Breaking news: he's alive. *Mind you, it wasn't easy for me to realize it. It took a while. What do you mean, you knew I was alive? That's crap, if you knew before I did.*

So, you're wondering why I told you I was dead? Firstly, because you didn't read it properly. I never said I was certain I was dead. I took 'oratory precautions', as they say when you bust a gut trying to speak like in a book on Greek mythology. I did say, I think. *And that was true. Honestly, I don't know where I was all that time. I told you, there were the lorry's headlights, then a sort of black hole, and I could definitely tell that, afterwards, I wasn't in real life any more. Even though I continued to think, to reflect. Like in a long dream, but without all the weird stuff. No images of me flying through the air doing backstroke, no three-headed ghost pursuing me down the corridors of Sleeping Beauty's castle, no sex with Jennifer Preston-Conwell – nothing, zilch,* niente, nada *– simply normal, everyday thoughts.*

You're quite rightly asking how I know I'm not dead. I'd like to tell you that I saw the tunnel, a white light, that God called me to Him, that He was beautiful, that He was big, that He had the fragrance of warm clouds, and that He said to me, 'Your time hasn't come, young Louis; go back down to Earth and don't come back for around a hundred years.' Except that, in reality, it wasn't at all like that. In reality, I was in my dreamworld-that-wasn't, I could no longer feel my body, I was no more than a spirit, a thought. No, I'm not mad, I promise you – I mean, I don't think I am – but you'll have sussed by now that you have to be wary of my I thinks.

So, I was in this other world, when, all of a sudden, I began to feel my body again. First of all, my fingers. My fingers became real again – I felt a horrible tingling. You know, like at night when you've slept too long on your arm, you feel as if you've got a piece of dead wood at the end of your body, your hand doesn't respond any more and you just have to wait for the pins and needles to pass, for the blood to start flowing back. Sometimes it tickles a bit; sometimes it hurts so much that you feel as if your arm's going to die. Well, I began to have this permanent sensation of fingers dying in a fire, being pricked by millions of pins and needles. Then I started feeling the same pain in different parts of my body, and I realized I was going to have to grin and bear it. Gradually, I got used to it. Or is it that it just became less intense? I'm not sure. What I was certain of, though, was that my body had woken up but couldn't move. Even though I concentrated as hard as I could, even though I instructed my eyelids to open, my hand to move, my tongue to wag, nothing happened. It was driving me nuts. I started to cry. To yell. In my head, of course. I was in a prison and I was alone. After battling for hours and hours (days?), I went back to sleep, I think. Then I woke up, I think. Then fell asleep again, I think. I'll spare you the details, but I think this little game went on for quite some time.

Then something weird happened. I heard someone talking. At first it was a vague, distant sound. I seriously started wondering whether I'd arrived in a beyond that neither Mum nor I had ever believed in. Then I said to myself that it was strange to welcome newcomers with, 'Have you done room 405 this morning, Brigitte?'

Oh my God. Oh my God. Oh my God. Oh my God. That's how people react when something crazy happens in an American TV series. In text-speak, people say, OMG. So I think I can hear OMG OMG OMG OMG all around me.

What conclusion should I draw from that?

Conclusion number one: I'm in room 405, or not far from room 405.

Conclusion number two: there are two people nearby, one of whom is a certain Brigitte. I don't know any Brigittes, apart from the band that sings 'Battez-vous' – 'Fight'. Was it a message, telling me to hang in there? Pretty complicated, if it is. Am I going to be entitled to a little private concert? I doubt it.

Conclusion number three: seeing as Brigitte replied from a distance that no, she hadn't done 405 yet, but there was no rush and it wasn't dirty, I guess it's about doing the cleaning in room 405.

I decided to wait a bit – so to speak, since I had no option. In the meantime, I listened out for the slightest sound. I was like Ali Baba entering the cave of wonders, like Harry Potter discovering his magic powers, like Cinderella dazzled by her coach, like . . . OK, you get the idea. Every sound was a jewel; I was all excited, even though I knew that nothing showed. From the outside, I must look super-poker-faced – the famous expressionless, unfathomable look of the professional bluffer. Apparently, I wasn't very expressive, that was the least that could be said. A quick analysis of the surrounding noises: regular beeps; breathing (mine, maybe); a vague din of voices and cutlery, like a far-off canteen; Brigitte's friend, who was humming a tune I didn't recognize, broke off and said, 'Good morning, doctor.' I'm in hospital. You knew that, too? Shit. So, if you know other things, tell me, because this is beginning to be a pain. Anyhow, I'm sure you didn't know I'd begun to hear again, seeing as I've only just discovered it myself.

Several people came into the room I'm in, and the sound level increased. A man's voice, two women's voices. New ones. I admit I didn't catch everything, but I understood a lot, all the same, and not only good things. They were talking about me; I heard my name several times. I gathered that my condition was stable. Not better, not worse. Nothing particular to say. Stable, how? That's when I heard the word. Coma. It was a shock. Coma means you're in a bad way. When, in a film, people are told,

He's in a coma, *they burst into tears, faint, scream or hit the doctor, who ends up seducing the grief-stricken mother.* I immediately thought about Mum. Did she know I was in a coma? Of course she knew. Had she already punched the doctor in the face? That would be just like her, and the thought made me smile – inwardly, of course; externally, I was poker-faced.

What stage of the coma drama were we at? I felt bad for Mum. Me, I hadn't known I was in a coma, so it wasn't so bad for me, after all. I wanted to know how long I'd been there, but, seeing as no one could hear me, there was no way of getting them to tell me. I concentrated very hard and, at one point, one of the ladies said, 'What day is it?' Tick-tock, tick-tock, I was going to find out. The other one replied, 'It's Thursday.' That didn't tell me much. Then she went on: 'The nineteenth of January.'

OMG. The last I knew, it was Saturday, 7 January. What had happened in the meantime? Now, I was beginning to seriously imagine what state Mum and Granny Odette must be in and I only wanted one thing: to tell them that I could hear again, that everything was going to be fine, that I would no doubt be able to speak to them soon.

I waited all day. I slept a little, thought a lot, listened a lot. I waited for Mum, I waited for Granny Odette.

When I heard someone say goodnight, in the corridor, I understood the day was over. No one had come to see me. I was on my own.

I began to cry.

Inwardly, of course; externally, I was poker-faced.

7

26 Days

WILLPOWER

It was another few days before I could face up to going into Louis's room. Not the one in the Robert Debré Hospital, the other one. His real room. Since 7 January, I hadn't been able to cross the threshold. I'd closed the door and hadn't opened it again. My mother had understood the importance of this room for my psychological healing, and hadn't set foot inside either, letting me take things at my own pace – for once.

One day, I felt ready. Ready to face the posters of his heroes, his drawings of his favourite idols, his unmade bed, his pyjamas scrunched into a ball and tossed on the desk, his homework book open at the page for Monday, 9 January. I stayed in his room for a long time. I tidied it slowly, carefully, and decided to wash his dirty bed linen. As I lifted the mattress to remove the sky-blue fitted sheet, I heard a thud. An object had just fallen out on to the wooden floor. I pulled the mattress towards me again, to see if there was anything else, but that was all. Then I knelt down and reached under the bed to pick up whatever it was that had dropped out.

It was a paperback A5 notebook, the cover of which was plastered with stickers of football stars. I smiled and opened it. On the flyleaf was written:

My Book of Wonders

The author of those words was my son. I recognized his cramped script, still awkward despite his age. A common trait in some bright children, I'd been told: their thoughts run ahead of their hand; their writing is often careless and rushed. Holding my breath, I turned the page and began reading.

My dearest Book of Wonders,

I'm making a list of all the things I'd like to experience before I die: my wonders. It's a sort of bucket list, except not really, because I've put things that I think are do-able.

It's an open-ended list. I'll add to it gradually, whenever I think of something, or someone, cool stuff or more intense stuff. Seeing as I don't plan to die straight away, I made sure you were nice and fat, my dearest, my precious Book of Wonders. It's Isa who gave me the idea. She's on the list. :-)

Sleep well, my little wonders!

Louis

I hadn't been expecting this. I closed the book and quickly put it on Louis's desk, as if it might burn my hands. I sat down on the stool facing the desk and continued to stare at it from a distance. Top scorer Antoine Griezmann was giving me a broad, toothy, reassuring smile. After reading the title on the flyleaf, I'd said to myself that Louis was going a bit over the top in describing these guys in shorts who chased after a ball as 'wonders'. I thought I was going to find the notebook full of pictures of footballers like the ones on the cover. Instead, I had just unearthed a little book of dreams, hidden under my son's mattress and mentioning a name I'd never heard. Who was this Isa? I felt as if I was intruding. It made me uncomfortable, as if I was entering a secret garden whose gate I'd kicked in. I immediately felt an irrepressible urge to cry, but I knew that my mother was within earshot, and I didn't want her bursting into Louis's room. I managed to hold back my tears. I closed the door. I wanted to be on my own.

I sat there for a long while. I was overwhelmed. What should I do? All I wanted to do was to read the rest. Turn the pages, explore Louis's private world, find out about the things that he most wanted to experience. And, more than anything, to find out whether I was in his Book of Wonders . . . like this Isa, of whom I was instantly jealous. Had my son included me in his fantasy future?

I didn't give in to the temptation to open the notebook. I decided to put it back where I'd found it and to think carefully about the right thing to do. I was very subdued during dinner. My mother noticed, of course – she always notices everything. I was afraid she'd go rummaging around in Louis's room the following night, so I pretended to be reading a book, of which I've never managed to get past page eight, and waited patiently for her to start snoring. Then I went and fetched the notebook and took it into my room. I spent several hours endlessly mulling over the problem, unable to make up my mind, then I fell asleep. I didn't read the contents; I just flicked through to see if it was full, and it was – or several pages were, at any rate.

In the middle of the night, I woke with a jolt. I'd had a strange dream. I was sitting beside Louis, in his bedroom at home. Louis yawned and closed his eyes, but I wouldn't let him fall asleep; I was reading to him and, whenever he was about to drop off, I called him to order. Then the room turned into a hospital room, and this time Louis *was* asleep. I was reading the same book to him, but he wasn't moving any more, he wasn't responding. I closed the book and acted out the scenes, but it had no effect on him. I carried on miming and I was growing older. When I reached sixty, Louis opened his eyes and let out a yell. I dropped the book and saw that it wasn't a novel or a collection of short stories. It was the notebook. I woke up in a sweat.

A little seed had been planted, a crazy idea was germinating in my mind. I had a fixed idea that was going round and round: *Louis isn't dead; he's in a coma, but he's alive. Thelma, anything is still possible, he's got nearly a month to wake up, he's going to wake up.* The medical team kept repeating that he was probably completely unconscious. Were they sure? No, they couldn't say so with certainty. So there was a chance that he could hear me, that he could feel me. I was going to hold on to that.

I had to make my son want to come back, entice him by showing him all the things he was missing out on by remaining in a coma. Make him want to live. It was a crazy idea, but do-able. I was convinced of it.

The players? A sportsman: Louis. A coach: me.

The challenge? Emerging from a coma, freestyle.

The prize? Everything that was written in the notebook. That notebook was a distillation of the future. That notebook was filled with things Louis dreamt of experiencing, promises of joy – of 'cool stuff', as he put it. That notebook was a promise of life.

The how? I was going to fulfil my son's dreams, experience them for him, make audio and video recordings and share them with him. I was going to take a solemn oath to do so. I couldn't go back, and I couldn't let him down. I didn't know whether there was a set order, and I wanted everything to be spontaneous. So I would have to discover the programme, bit by bit.

The goal? That my son would say, *Shit, I can't have my mum doing all that instead of me.* And for him to open his eyes.

I shuddered. I got up and looked out of the window, at the sky. Was I going mad? In the space of a few seconds, I had dispelled the dark clouds hanging over my son. But the blackness was dense, the outcome uncertain. Louis might never come back, I knew that. I began to cry silently, motionless. My determination was probably absurd, but I couldn't resign myself to letting my son go, without having enabled him to fulfil all his childhood dreams.

How much time did I have left? Less than a month, now. I'd already lost precious days. It was more than time to start this desperate race for life.

I turned the first page and found out what lay in store for me.

I was going to leave my comfort zone, I knew. I was ready.

For Louis. But a little for myself too.

25 Days

TOKYO'S A VERY LONG WAY

After a sleepless night, I packed my suitcase and booked a flight to Tokyo at an exorbitant price. The only seats available were in business class, but, given my lawyer's latest update on the negotiations with Hégémonie, I could even have treated myself to first.

I arrived at the hospital at dawn that day and, before I dropped in to say goodbye to Louis, I made a pact with Sophie Davant. She listened to me earnestly, staring at me as if I were an alien. Then she burst out laughing and told me that my idea was brilliant, and that of course she'd help me as much as she could. I hugged her, which surprised her, but she didn't object. She asked if she could tell the other nurses, especially her friend who's the spitting image of the TV presenter Catherine Laborde (you couldn't make that up). I agreed, telling myself that this friendship between the two channels, TF1 and France Télévisions, augured well for my scheme, which relied heavily on audiovisual technology. I'd stuffed Louis's mini action camera into my handbag, and I planned to study the instructions on the plane. Tokyo's a very long way, and the twelve-hour flight would give me time to become a professional camerawoman. At least that's what I told myself then, blithely unaware how totally useless I would be at film editing.

I explained to Louis the crazy project that had formed in my mind. My son remained beautiful, calm and still, but that morning something unusual happened. I knew my son inside out, and since he'd been in that hospital bed, nothing of his expression was new to me. I could describe his fine nose, his hairline, his delicate eyelids in perfect detail, and his eyebrows, which I smoothed each time the nurses washed his face. After telling him my plans for the coming weeks, my heart contracted and lurched at the same time. In the corner of Louis's right eye, a tear welled up and then ran down his temple. Louis was crying, I was convinced. My heart began pounding, and I gave a shout, which brought two nurses rushing in. I wanted to share my excitement, have them bear witness: something had just happened on my son's face! But the bubble burst. One of the nurses, one I didn't like, and whose name and face I kept forgetting (each time, I would catch myself asking who she was, before recognizing her), snapped back that this sort of thing sometimes happened, that it was certainly not a tear, but perhaps a drop of water on his eyelid from when his face had been washed not long before, or a secretion, which meant nothing. 'Your son's readings are still unchanged, I'm very sorry, madame.' I sat down and gazed fixedly at Louis. Waiting for more. Cry, please, my darling. Show them I'm not mad. Show them you're fighting.

I so longed for him to wake up. I was determined to fight, as long as there was breath in my lungs and in his. I'd made that irreversible decision the day after the pronouncement made by Dr Beaugrand. Actually, that decision had always been inside me, since the accident. But I'd had to be shaken up by my own mother, and especially by the ominous countdown, for it to appear as blindingly obvious to me. I had to stop wallowing in self-pity and blame, and grasp hope by the horns and not let go again.

*

At 20:35, a few metres from the plane, I was still wondering how to conduct myself. Of course, I was convinced that the mission I'd just signed up for was the right thing to do. Of course, I was excited at the thought of what lay in store, and the journey ahead, both physical and emotional. Of course, I also knew that my mother would be there for my son. But no longer being able to touch him or kiss him during the coming days felt like a cruel deprivation. I was terrified that his condition might deteriorate during my absence.

My mother – who hadn't let me out of her sight over the past few days – had sensed my twitchiness, but I'd managed to keep my discovery and my decision from her. Nothing horrified me more than the prospect of having a minder shadowing me.

I waited for the last call for boarding and checked that I had the precious little notebook with me, opening my handbag and stroking the laminated cover celebrating Neymar, and I finally made my way towards the flight attendant.

Deep breath, big smile, settle into seat 6A. I couldn't believe the size of the seat, and didn't understand how to turn it into a bed (this was the first time I'd travelled in business class). I marvelled at the little warm towel, friendly smiles from the cabin crew, the glass of champagne that I could enjoy without being reprimanded by my mother, who was subjecting me to a food hell, including total abstinence from alcohol, since she'd scraped me off the floor the night of Dr Beaugrand's pronouncement. I relished the feeling of being pampered.

I felt good, just good. I hadn't felt like that for seventeen days. No, on second thoughts, for much longer.

I raised my glass. To your dreams, my son.

2

The Book of Wonders

9

24 Days

JUMPING INTO THE VOID

Arigatou gozaimasu!

'Ar-i-ga-too . . . gauze-eye-massu!'

This language is hellishly difficult. Even with my pocket idiot's guide to Japanese in my right hand, I couldn't work out the sounds. On the plane, I'd tried to mug up on essential phrases like this polite 'thank you', which is used for just about everything, but I'd fallen asleep. Obviously, a night flight takes place during the night, as its name suggests. I should have realized that I'd set myself too many goals and that the combined effect of the champagne and exhaustion would mean that I'd sleep for half the flight. At least I was on form for the evening. With an eight-hour time difference, I was just waking up, but the sun was already setting over Tokyo.

At the airport, all the signs were in English. After collecting my luggage and withdrawing several thousand yen from the A.T.M., I easily found a taxi. I showed the driver the address of my hotel on my smartphone;

he nodded and we drove for around forty minutes. Already the taxi was a novel experience. I thought this first taxi was an exception, but I soon found out that it was the rule. The driver wore white gloves and was dressed as if for a wedding. There was a transparent partition with an intercom between him and the passenger compartment. He handed me a moist towel in a plastic sachet. The seats had lacy covers worthy of my grandmother. A bit outlandish, kitsch, aseptic – a real culture shock.

I immediately thought of Louis, of his passion for Japanese cartoons. It was perfectly logical for his list of wonders to begin with Tokyo. He'd asked me several times to take him there, but I hadn't found a moment to do so. Too much work, holidays reduced to the bare minimum. There, in that Tokyo taxi smelling strongly of cheap perfume, I promised myself I'd take him to Japan. For real.

I'd chosen a luxury hotel which a rapid online search told me was an absolute must. *If Sofia Coppola's film* Lost in Translation *had been shot in 2017, it would have been in this establishment, without any doubt*, an influential blogger had written. A compelling argument, which had convinced me. It wasn't exactly cheap, but from the minute I set foot inside, I had no regrets. The hotel was in a quiet neighbourhood – Toranomon Hills – between the fortieth and sixtieth floors of a skyscraper that overlooked the city, and had an extraordinary view of Tokyo Tower, the red and white copy of the Eiffel Tower. The designer lobby was sophisticated and refined, highly original. Grandiose. I was beginning to feel feverish with excitement, telling myself I was going to love Tokyo.

My room was stunning. One entire wall was a floor-to-ceiling window. I was on the forty-seventh floor and I had the sensation of being immersed in the city. No buildings in my sight line, just a dizzying panorama. I turned off the lights in the room so as not to have the view spoilt by any reflections. Night had fallen, the city's lights twinkled some dozens of metres below me. I had never experienced anything like it. Of course, I'd already been to the top of the Tour Montparnasse in Paris, but then I'd been in a throng of tourists, with cameras flashing and hysterical shrieks. Here, I was alone, in the pitch dark, in utter silence. I pressed myself up against the glass and gazed out avidly.

I thought about Amélie Nothomb. In her novel *Fear and Trembling*, she describes so well that incredible sensation of throwing oneself into the view, the giddy appeal of the endless space. She talks about 'mental defenestration' – that intoxicating feeling of jumping into the void. I was experiencing it, I could feel the heartbeat of this unknown city.

I switched on Louis's camera and filmed for several

73

minutes, describing as much as I could aloud. 'You have to come and see this, darling. Thank you for bringing me here.'

How long did I stay like that? Long enough, in any case, to be able to tick off one of the wonders that Louis had listed:

Admire the lights of Tokyo from the top of a skyscraper.

I was so entranced by the beauty of the place that, in the end, I decided to spend my evening at the hotel. The top floor was given over to a swimming pool, which was also completely crazy. All the walls were glass and I was able to 'mentally defenestrate' at leisure, my feet dangling in the water, sipping a hot tea. For a moment, I felt as if I had touched paradise on Earth with my finger. Only for a moment.

Later, I dined in the restaurant, three floors below, which afforded the same breathtaking view. Since my arrival a few hours earlier, I'd kept telling myself that it was actually nice to be alone, that I could organize my time as I pleased. I don't know if I really thought that or whether I was trying to convince myself. Because, having dinner on the top of the city, in the company of my Tokyo guidebooks, surrounded by couples enjoying a romantic dinner, I suddenly felt uncomfortable. I gazed around the room to check whether mine was the only table for one. There was another, at the other end of the restaurant. My pride was saved. A man, apparently, from the look of his clothes and his shape. But, from so far away and with the subdued lighting, it was hard to tell.

I got up and went to the toilet. Japanese toilets: another experience on Louis's list, which I'd already ticked off in my room. Louis had written:

Press all the buttons on a Japanese toilet.

To be honest, I wasn't mad about the warm seat or the little jet aimed at my bottom. I've always been afraid of toilets with any kind of electronic component. I suspect they rarely malfunction, but, even so, I'm always afraid that something will go wrong, that the jet is angled badly and will hit my face – horror of horrors – or drench my blouse. In other words, I far prefer my old Parisian loo.

On the way back to my table, I glanced at the lone man I'd spotted from a distance, and froze. It wasn't a man. I drew closer and let out a strangled cry, which echoed in that hushed atmosphere.

'Mum? What are you doing here?'

'Hello, darling. What an amazing place, isn't it?'

'You haven't answered my question. What the fuck are you doing here, Mum? How did you know I was here?'

'You underestimate me, my little pussycat. I have my methods, you know. You should be more discreet when you tell the nurses about your plans, and also more creative in making up email passwords. Excellent choice of hotel, in any case.'

My mother is a geek. An I.T. junkie. She's sixty, but she's way better at it than I am. That's one of the reasons why Louis has always adored her. *A geeky granny – that's so cool*, he's forever saying. I think it's the pits.

'Mum, you can't afford a hotel like this, or such a trip; what are you playing at?'

'I have to say that the twelve-hour flight in economy gave me such a stiff neck . . . I envied you in business class!'

'You mean you were on the same flight?'

'Of course, pussycat. I checked in at the last minute; luckily, there were a few no-shows, so I managed to get a seat. I told you I wouldn't let you out of my sight, and now I've promised Louis too. But you're right, I can't afford this hotel . . . Luckily, I'm your guest.'

'I beg your pardon?'

'The nice young man at reception took my luggage up to your room and gave me a key. Don't forget we have the same surname. I simply mentioned that I was a little late, that my darling daughter had already gone up to the room we're sharing. I gave him my passport and that did the trick. I said all that in English, with my dreadful accent – you'd have been proud of me. Don't worry, I'll keep out of your way.'

That was how I found myself sharing my queen-size bed and my dream room with my mother, her eccentricities and her loud snores.

Mum Rocks

I love it, I love it, I love it, I love it, I love it, I love it.

I still find it hard to believe, but I totally love my mother's idea.

When she came to tell me about it, I must say I went through a whole bunch of conflicting feelings. At first, I felt all weird. She told me she wouldn't judge what I'd written in the notebook, that, if it was there, she'd do it. That she was going to inspire me to surpass myself, so I could join her and live all my dreams. If I hadn't been in this condition, I'd have said no, for sure. My notebook is a private thing. But, seeing as I couldn't protest, I listened to her. And, in the end, I told myself that she must love me to bits to do that. It did me good to feel her emotion and hear her talk the way she did. She's never spoken to me like that before. But I felt bad for her, too. I told myself that she must be suffering terribly. I understood that she'd made a big scene and quit Hégémonie and was going to get a load of dosh, but I know how much her career means to her, so I pictured her moping, alone, in the living room, and I felt bad. Immediately after, I could hear Grandma saying, 'Pull yourself together, for pity's sake, don't let yourself go. Have you finished feeling sorry for yourself?' (yes, Granny Odette says, 'for pity's sake', 'poppycock' and 'shhh ... sugar', and a whole load of expressions from two hundred years ago), and that made me smile again, and I kept on smiling because I started to imagine Mum living my dreams.

The things I'd written in the notebook slowly started coming back to me, and just picturing her in some of those situations made me laugh myself silly. Inwardly, of course. Outwardly, still poker-faced. Well, not as poker-faced as all that. I kept bursting out in silent laughter, and, at one point, Mum interrupted my laughing fit by letting out a shriek. Apparently, I'd shed a tear. For me, too, that was insane. Were the nurses right – had Mum imagined it? Or had my manic inner laughter triggered a visible reaction? I felt a sort of rush of hope and joy. It lasted all day, and has stayed with me ever since.

I heard Mum explain her idea to Charlotte, her favourite nurse, who she always calls Sophie Davant – so that I can visualize her, she says, even though I've never heard of Sophie Davant. Charlotte was helpless with laughter too, and Mum has given her an iPad so she can send me videos from Japan, since she's starting with my first challenge, the one in Tokyo. I say 'challenge' because I know that my dreams can easily turn into Mum's Ultimate Survival ordeal. And that's what's so brilliant.

The disappointment of 19 January, that first day when I was conscious but no one came to see me – I can tell you I'm over that. I know now that Mum's there, and she's fighting. I know that Grandma's there too. Oh, and I must tell you about the best bit, which made me laugh my socks off. A few minutes after Mum left, Granny Odette came to see me. She chatted innocently to Charlotte/Sophie Davant, but I could tell she was plotting something. She acted like she was in on Mum's plans, whereas I knew she hadn't the faintest idea. Grandma's crafty. So Charlotte told her everything, in the most natural way, and Grandma took in the information in the most natural way too.

When Charlotte left the room, Grandma came over and whispered that there was no way she was going to let Mum go off on her own to such an unfamiliar, faraway country, that she was sorry to have to leave me for a few days, but she was sure I understood. That of course I mustn't breathe a word to Mum, but she was going to follow her from a distance. You can trust me, Grandma; I'll be as silent as the grave. Excuse the pun, but Grandma just kills me. If I'd been my usual self, I'd have had a bellyache from laughing so much all day. I'd love to be a fly on the wall, just to see Mum's face when Grandma rocks up.

I love my mum to bits, I love my grandma to bits – they're the best. I can't wait to hear about their Tokyo trip; they're really going to kick ass.

10

23 Days

ALL ABOUT MY MOTHER

Unable to sleep because of jet lag and the strange sounds coming from my bedfellow, I lay awake all night, thinking. About my life. About my mother. About us.

For as long as I could remember, I'd been Thelma the pseudo-rebel, fighting against everything for the sake of it. I wasn't named after Thelma in the 1990s film *Thelma and Louise* – I'm much too old for that. I was born in 1977, when Thelma Houston was topping the charts with the mega international hit 'Don't Leave Me This Way', which my mother, Odette, was crazy about. These days, of course, when I tell people my name, they always think of the film with Susan Sarandon and Geena Davis. When Ridley Scott's film was released, it blew me away. A starstruck teenager, I identified with the story of those two strong and sexy women. They became my role models, a sort of feminine ideal. I'd never believed in God, and I saw the film as a sign from destiny: now my name was associated with a symbol that was much more meaningful than an old forty-five-r.p.m. record. I know the film ends in tragedy, but the impact it had on me was positive. Thelma and Louise are symbols of women's freedom of choice, of women who owe men nothing, have no expectations of them and get by on their own.

When I fell pregnant, I decided to keep the baby, knowing that I would raise it without a father. I hoped to have a girl and call her Louise. But Louise turned out to be a boy. That's the way it is, and I'm very glad. Louis is the only male who matters to me.

My mother brought me up alone too. Odette is a product of May '68, who's always campaigned to do as she pleases with her body, for her freedom of thought, and I admired her for that. I grew up with the idealized memory of an absent father, who'd died during a demonstration against the destruction of the steel industry. I wasn't yet a year old, and the figure of that untouchable, irreplaceable father swept away all hope of a family life. My mother continued his work as a union activist, and, as far back as I can remember, I've always seen her involved in the struggle. She left no door open in her life for a man. She drowned her grief in her battles, and her day-to-day work as a primary-school teacher and activist in an education priority zone. Success for all, darling. I was full of admiration for her! I spent so much time marching in the streets with her! I remember the May Day parades – first of all on her shoulders, a few years later holding one end of a banner, then my own flag. I was proud of her, proud of myself, proud to honour my father's memory.

Then came my teens. My anxieties, my embarrassment, my aching desire to fit in, to be a slave like everyone else to the fashion brands, American princes and princesses, stereotyped beauty. I was fed up with shapeless jumpers with a picture of Che Guevara on them, having Mum cut my hair, tatty trainers, rejection of the capitalist world. I hated the alternative lifestyle that prevented me from being accepted by the cool girls at school, made me a laughing-stock among the boys of my age, so sexy in their Nike Air Jordans, baggy Poivre Blanc sweaters and Adidas tracksuit bottoms, unzipped at the ankles.

I didn't understand my mother's wholesale rejection of all that; I resented her for denying me a normal life. So I started loathing her violently, and automatically doing the opposite of what she wanted for me. I hated her lanky, pipe-cleaner look, her bandy legs in her loose-fitting, worn jeans, the way she smoked her cigarettes, holding them between her thumb and forefinger, her ashen hair clipped back in that eternal tone-on-tone grip, her cowboy whistles, her hard expression and her disparaging words, her disapproval of my lifestyle. I did my utmost to become everything she abhorred. She saw me as an irresponsible mother, wasting the best years of my life pursuing my career, obsessed with the sales figures of a multinational corporation that had no qualms about outsourcing overseas and selling products that were purely frivolous.

The only bond we still have is Louis. Louis has always been allowed to see his grandmother whenever he wants to. Always. A matter of principle, of roots. And the three of us have brunch together once a month. Which is what we were supposed to have been doing on that fateful Saturday, 7 January.

After my long and intense night of thinking, I finally decided to accept my lot. My mother was there, with me, 10,000 kilometres from Paris. And I'd promised Louis I'd carry out what was written in his little Book of Wonders, to the letter.

He'd drawn up a detailed list of things he wanted to experience in Japan, the title of which said it all:

Have a wild day in Tokyo with the person I love more than anyone else in the world (Mum, for the time being).

I found the 'for the time being' a bit disconcerting. I managed to take it on the chin, but the mere idea that he could think that one day he might love someone more than me had wounded my broken little heart – and my strong ego. Then I remembered that, when I was his age, I couldn't have foreseen that he would come along and I'd love him more than anyone else, so I swallowed my pride and moved on. I had initially thought I'd be ticking the box alone, since I was not going to be able to spend my 'wild day' in Tokyo with 'the person I love more than anyone else in the world' – in other words, Louis. On second thoughts, it was bending the rules of the game. Louis had stipulated that the challenges had to be experienced by two people – that was what he meant. But, apart from Louis, there was no one I really loved ... Sad, I know, but that's the way things were. The next person on my list of potential people I loved was my mother, I had to admit it.

There, lying in that vast bed, closer to her than I had been since I was fourteen, I became aware of the emptiness of that 'list of people I love'. I wasn't antisocial, I had lots of acquaintances with whom I enjoyed a good night out, but I didn't really have any friends. Love and friendship required an effort which I'd given up on a long time ago, when I left Louis's father, before he knew he was going to be a father. Since the accident, I could count on the fingers of one hand the people who'd tried to get in touch to find out how I was. I hadn't called them back. I'd got lots of friends on Facebook, lots of real-life men and women mates, but no true friends. I hadn't been unhappy about it; it was my choice. My priorities had always been clear: raise my son and have a successful career.

My Aunt Odile never had children, much to her regret. My only family, right now, were Louis and my mother. I sat up in bed. We'd left the curtains open and the white light of the city bathed the room in a ghostly glow. I watched my mother sleeping. She seemed peaceful. Her face less stern than when she was awake. I found her beautiful. An unconventional beauty – angular, obstinate. I lay back down and continued to look at her. I told myself that ultimately Louis would no doubt be delighted if I spent this wished-for 'wild day' with his grandmother.

When she woke up, and I suggested it, I saw a new glint in her steel-blue eyes. She hadn't been expecting this. She had probably been planning to follow me like a secret agent, complaining about those 'darn Japanese', cursing me out loud, and here I was offering her a completely different prospect. She merely said, 'Thank you,' looked down to hide her emotion, then said, 'So, what do we start with?' I told her that I hoped she had a strong stomach, because we had a lot on our plate. She gave a gleeful laugh that I found completely unrecognizable.

And we went out into the singular warmth of that winter's day in Tokyo.

11

23 to 22 Days

MY MOTHER AS A MAID
IN A KARAOKE CLUB

'Anniiiiie aime les sucettes, les sucettes à l'anis . . .'

We were in a karaoke bar in Shibuya, the trendy district that never sleeps, and I think the surreal image of my mother, dressed up as a saucy maid, screeching France Gall's cute Lolita number about loving lollipops, a song which she hates, surrounded by Japanese in high spirits, chorusing *'Kanpai!'* at the end of every line, will remain etched in my memory forever.

Naturally, it occurred to me to capture that magic moment for posterity. I had difficulty filming because I was in fits of giggles, which made the camera wobble. At one point, one of our fellow drinkers grabbed the camera, and his friends gave me a second mic and pushed me on to the mini stage. My mother, who generally doesn't drink and who'd been downing glasses of *umeshu* – a moreish plum liqueur – yelled that she was very happy to sing this duet with me, grabbing me by the neck, like a drunkard at a village beer festival in Alsace, and shrieking even louder when Johnny

Hallyday's 'Que je t'aime' came on. That night, we discovered that Japanese karaoke bars, as well as being places of wild drinking, are veritable museums of international music hits, and that the French pop songs of the Sixties to the Nineties are a big favourite.

The day had begun a great deal more calmly. We'd followed Louis's plan to the letter, and I piqued my mother's curiosity by disclosing each stage only as we came to it. So, for her, the day had been a series of surprises. It was the first time she'd been outside Europe, and only her third time out of France, and she was like a kid, impatient to find out what was next. She relied on me, because I both had the schedule and spoke English – for want of Japanese – and I had the feeling that our roles had been reversed: I was the mother, travelling with her child who was carrying a senior citizen's card.

The first stage was the Pokémon Center megastore, in Ikebukuro, where we bought thirty or so *super-rare* cards and posed in front of giant statues of Pikachu and his friends. People dressed as strange creatures, in cosplay outfits, greeted us: teenagers disguised as characters from the Studio Ghibli, candyfloss-pink schoolgirls, punk Lolitas, superheroes going around in noisy groups. I recognized a Sailor Moon, two Hello Kittys, a Totoro and a few Pokémon heroes, but I'm certain that Louis would have identified most of the characters.

Next, we went for a stroll in the vast gardens around

the Meiji Jingu. We were awestruck by this oasis of nature and history in the heart of the city's hustle and bustle. A surprising change of scene. We gave in to the temptation of taking a selfie in front of the majestic collection of ancient sake barrels that greets visitors, then we captured the special atmosphere of the shrine by placing the camera on a low wall for some minutes. Louis would be able to listen at leisure to the special peacefulness of Tokyo's nature, the murmur of the city providing a subtle soundscape. The foreground was made up of birds twittering and rustling foliage. We stayed there for a long time, listening. Waiting for the next step of our adventure.

A traditional wedding was going to be celebrated at the Meiji Jingu. I had no idea why Louis wanted to attend a Japanese wedding; it was most likely something he'd read about in a manga magazine, the extraordinary beauty of which he'd intuited. The procession approached. I gestured to the bride to ask if we could film, and she agreed with a smile. She seemed to be imbued with the magic of the Meiji Jingu and of the moment, utterly still in her immaculate cocoon-like dress, a chrysalis of purity. Time was suspended in the reds of the kimonos, the copper roofs, the slow, coordinated steps, the weight of tradition. Leaning towards the camera, I quietly described the scene, mindful of the solemnity of the moment: 'It's a stunning sight, darling. You have to see it for yourself. Thank you for having brought us here.'

After this moving interlude, we decided to dive straight into the buzzing Shibuya district. Shibuya – everyone knows it, without knowing it. It's that crazy intersection, with a tangle of pedestrian crossings and tall buildings covered in giant screens, screaming noise and lights. The Japanese Times Square. I'd read that this legendary crossing is the epitome of Japanese discipline: when the lights change to green for pedestrians, hundreds of people cross at the same time, carefully avoiding one another. 'Imagine what chaos it would be if Parisians were thrown in there,' Mum remarked with her usual tact. She couldn't have spoken a truer word. I was a little afraid of what Louis had planned, but I had to follow everything to the letter. *We* had to follow everything to the letter.

We waited by one of the pedestrian crossings, surrounded by a hundred or so people. A hundred or so others stood facing us. Ignoring her protests, I attached Louis's camera to my mother's forehead with a 'Take it or leave it' that made her laugh and mutter that the apple doesn't fall far from the tree and that I was well and truly my mother's daughter. I switched on the camera and took her wrinkled palm in mine.

'On the count of three, we close our eyes.'

'You're joking, I hope? Are you trying to kill me, or what?'

'On the count of three, we close our eyes, Mum.'

'Mary, mother of Jesus, what have I done for God to punish me like this–?'

'Mum, you've never believed in God!'

'Maybe that explains it.'

I laughed, and she laughed. I said, 'One, two, three – close your eyes!'

The pedestrian light must have turned green, because we surged forward with the crowd, our eyes closed. My mother yelped in a panic each time someone brushed against her, and I laughed all the more. Then my foot hit what must have been a kerb, I stumbled and Mum steadied me. I regained my balance, and we opened our eyes again. We were on the other side. We'd just crossed the busiest intersection in the world with our eyes closed, and not been jostled once. These Japanese were disarmingly disciplined and well mannered. We looked at one another and burst out laughing. I think we felt alive.

We decided to take a well-earned break in a café overlooking the Shibuya Crossing, watching (and filming) the ballet of pedestrians for some time, with what we guessed were the latest Japanese hits playing in the background. Dusk was about to fall and we hadn't noticed the time go by. It was already almost five and we still had a lot to do.

We took a taxi to the Shinjuku district, the hub of Tokyo nightlife, where I'd read you had to be careful. In the heart of Kabukicho, the red-light district where gaming rooms, hostess bars, restaurants, jazz clubs and meetings of the yakuza – the local mobsters – mingle, it was better not to follow just any person, anywhere. We dived headlong into the bustle, the crowd, the vertical luminous signs with incomprehensible ideograms. After locating – with difficulty – the address on Louis's list, which was very precise, when it came to Tokyo, we found ourselves in the waiting room of Tomohiro Tomoaki, alias Tomo: the celebrities' tattoo artist. I had to ask him to ink a part of my body, in order to check off this item on my son's motley Japanese wish list.

The walls were covered with photos of international stars proudly posing, one with an eagle on their hip, another with a greedy mouth at the top of their pubis (really classy – I won't reveal who it was, even under torture) . . . and I started to wonder what I'd got myself into. Mum was having fun acting the interviewer, filming me while asking me what it was like to be on the point of getting a penis tattoo on my right cheek – 'You never know what you'll end up with, with your level of Japanese.' Ha, ha, very funny. I'd decided to be restrained and have a plain capital L tattooed on the inside of my left wrist. It would be hidden by my watch most of the time.

I closed my eyes while Tomo was tattooing me and, in the end, I was very pleased with the result. Bearable pain, a discreet and beautiful Japanese-style L. We thanked him with a reverential bow that was probably inappropriate – I don't think I'll ever understand the complex codes of Japanese greetings – and emerged into the turmoil of Kabukicho.

After drinking a first *umeshu* in the Golden Gai district, full of microhouses concealing bars which can only cram in five or six people, we entered an *izakaya* – a traditional restaurant. We removed our shoes and sat on the floor, kneeling on a tatami. Our adventures had given us an appetite. Next on Louis's list was an exciting and scary command:

Eat in an izakaya, *ask for a menu in Japanese, with no photos, order five random dishes and eat them all!*

'You can count me out, pussycat. After all, you're the one who must follow Louis's instructions, not me.'

'You've got a nerve, Mum! If you decide you're going to be my guest – well, you're my guest to the end! Come on, let's both have another *umeshu* – that'll perk you up!'

My mother raised her eyes to the heavens, feigning exasperation with a broad smile, and answered in her best accent: 'Go for the oo-me-shoe . . .'

We ordered from a waiter who didn't speak a word of English, pointing to indecipherable words on the menu. As we made our choices, the waiter sometimes asked questions, sounding surprised – a rather unobtrusive Japanese surprise. Of course, we understood nothing and nodded foolishly while clucking like two impatient hens. I felt as

93

if I was Obelix, waiting for the dishes of Mannekenpix, the chef who cooked meals for the Titans, as I buckled down to one of the many tasks concocted by my son.

Various fish and shellfish sushi soon appeared on our table: we identified salmon, tuna, eel, fish roe (but what kind?), as well as a type of octopus. We didn't recognize a slightly sharp-tasting white fish, nor a viscous shell-fish. Then came a large noodle soup that we gathered was called *udon*, with shrimp fritters, mysterious vegetables, fried tofu and seaweed. So far, so good. Then we were served a bowl of plain rice, which on closer inspection turned out to be dotted with tiny whole fried fish, including the eyes. My mother protested, but we ate everything (and crunched, because those little fish were crispy), wincing as we did so.

The pièce de résistance was served by the chef himself. He came to our table with a live squid in his left hand and a large knife in his right. We stopped laughing like silly geese and the booming chef gratified us with an incomprehensible speech as he laid the creature on a wooden board. Then he calmly sliced it, placing the thin transparent strips in small bowls. Mum looked away; I laughed and pointed out that, since she ate live oysters, she could try the 'almost live' squid. Then the chef stood there in front of us. We thanked him, but he didn't leave. He was obviously waiting for us to try it. We had no option. I grabbed the camera and caught my mother's grimace and gag reflex as she put a piece of quivering squid in her mouth.

We washed it all down with some sake, then squandered a few thousand yen (a few tens of euros) in a smoke-filled *pachinko* – a sort of jam-packed casino, echoing with the sound of jangling, flashing machines, where thousands of workers seeking an adrenaline rush come to forget the emptiness of their lives. To round off our foray into Shinjuku in style, we tried a beer with wasabi at the Robot Restaurant, watching a cabaret show that was a cross between an episode of *Bioman* on speed, a cardboard cut-out parody of an American musical, and a Bollywood movie with ear-piercing singing, dancing and screeching.

Back in Shibuya, we joined a bunch of particularly tipsy Japanese for this group karaoke, and competed singing Eurovision songs and wearing absurd costumes.

I had to support my mother on the way back to the hotel – she could no longer walk straight – and the receptionist welcomed us with a smile in which I could discern a hint of anxiety.

'Everything's fine, don't worry. Goodnight.'

It was four o'clock in the morning. I lay Mum on the bed and removed her socks and the maid's hat she had forgotten to return with the rest of her costume. I 'mentally defenestrated' myself one last time, then I too lay down.

In seeking to awaken my son, I fell asleep, a little girl snuggled up to her mother.

Excerpt from the Book of Wonders

Have a wild day in Tokyo with the person I love more than any-one else in the world (Mum, for the time being).

– Raid the Pokémon Center in Ikebukuro for super-rare cards

– See a traditional wedding at the Meiji Jingu (with kimonos and the works)

– Let myself be swept along by the crowd on the Shibuya Crossing, with my eyes closed

– Get a tattoo from Tomo, tattooist to the stars (address: Tōkyō-to, Shinjuku-ku, Kabukichō, 1 Chome–12–2)

– Eat at an izakaya, ask for the menu in Japanese, with no pictures, and order five random dishes. And eat everything! Yum, yum!

– Press all the buttons on a Japanese toilet

– Blow my mind at the Robot Restaurant, Shinjuku

– Have a drink in the Golden Gai

– Burst my eardrums in a pachinko

– Sing my heart out in a karaoke bar in Shibuya

– Gaze at Tokyo's lights from the top of a skyscraper

I Dare

21 to 17 Days

Charlotte has nicknamed room 405 'the room of wonders', and that's what everyone calls it now. Since Mum rocked up with her sound system and spent a whole afternoon playing the videos and telling me about everything she filmed with Granny Odette in Tokyo, she's become a celebrity throughout the hospital.

Charlotte (who now has a name, so Mum no longer calls her Sophie Davant) told her that she'd love to see the video and so Mum chose a day when she was off duty. Of course, Charlotte knew all about the trip, because she'd played me loads of excerpts on the iPad, but she said she'd still love to attend the show. During the afternoon, other nurses, auxiliaries and medical secretaries wandered in and out when they were on a break, all of them laughing delightedly and saying thank you. At the end, Charlotte said to Mum, 'What you're doing for your son is amazing,' and I totally agree with her.

I had a great laugh, all afternoon, and I so wish I could have seen it! On video, but also for real. What I loved best was the unintentional Mum-and-Grandma comedy duo, a sort of female Laurel and Hardy, with cheap gags and old-lady humour. I loved it, and I'm not the only one, judging by the applause from the improvised audience. Grandma was there too, for the screening, and I had the feeling that something had happened between the two of them, over there. They were . . . How can I describe it? Complicit, I think. I'd never heard them like that. Apparently, it's Grandma who edited the videos, because Mum doesn't have a clue and Grandma's an I.T. whizz, but I can tell you she didn't censor anything. It's incredible. I want to get up and shout, Guys, that's my mum and my grandma, and they rock!!!

Then Mum stayed with me on her own, and she kissed me and kissed me, I think, then turned the next page of my Book of Wonders. She read what was written, and she nearly wet herself. At first, I was a bit ashamed because there were things that were a bit sexual, but Mum told me that she'd find some way of fulfilling my dreams, even if she didn't entirely approve. It was Sunday, 29 January; she gave herself two days, scout's honour (though she never was one). Seeing what I was about to make her do, it would be good if I could give her a sign.

'My darling, I love you, I miss you, and so does your grandmother,' she said. 'Come back quickly; I'm doing all this for you, to show you how beautiful life is, how much you have to live for.'

I promise, Mum, I'm going to try. You have no idea how much I want to.

The next evening, Mum told me about her first escapade. I have to say, I was blown away. I'd never have believed she'd do stuff like that. Best of all, she sounded as if she'd got a real buzz out of it and had a wicked time doing the stupid things I'd written on the page I'd called 'I dare' . . . A whole list.

She started with the easiest one on the list, or, at any rate, the least challenging. It was to get into a taxi and then act totally crazy and yell 'Follow that car!' like in spy films. I've always thought that sounded super cool and I've always fantasized about saying it for real. Well, my mother did it – three times, because the first two were disastrous: she was booted out of the cab within seconds. But the third attempt worked. She had the bright idea of yelling 'Police!' first, and of printing and laminating a fake ID which could fool someone who didn't look too closely, was stressed out by the urgency, or a bit of both. She flung herself into a taxi, brandished her ID and barked the words, totally into the role – eat your heart out, drama school, as she said. The driver shot off. He soon started asking questions, but she was prepared. Who were they following? Dangerous bank robbers. Why was she alone, when police officers always work in pairs? That was odd, wasn't it? She'd infiltrated the gang, backup was on its way. Then the questions became more precise. Which branch of the police was she in? The fraud squad . . . Robbery prevention. He hadn't heard of that department. Of course not, it had only recently been set up. Could he have her name and rank? She'd been caught off guard and had replied without thinking: 'Superintendent Adamsberg.' The driver was a crime-fiction fan and recognized the name of Fred Vargas's hero. He slammed the brakes on and ordered her out of his taxi, otherwise he'd call the police – the real police. She obeyed.

Even so, she'd had time to take a selfie inside the taxi, holding her ID, to capture the moment for me. I'd see that freaking photo when I could be bothered to open my eyes. I sensed a slight rebuke in that last sentence, which I put down to tiredness.

On Wednesday, 1 February, Mum came to see me with Grandma, to tell me about their adventures. The previous day, Mum had taken Grandma with her to 'film the ticking off of two boxes'. At first, I hadn't understood what she meant, but when she started playing the video on her iPad, I got it, and I felt as if I'd been there. They'd gone to the trouble of commentating on everything that was going on, to avoid leaving things unsaid . . . They were becoming real audio-description pros. To help you understand what follows, let me explain that the dialogue is between Madame Ernest, my maths teacher, and my mother. Grandma was holding the camera. Selected excerpts of what I heard:

'Thank you for seeing me and agreeing to be filmed, Madame Ernest. It means a lot to us.'

'You're very welcome. I was deeply saddened when I heard about your son. I hope he pulls through.'

'You can speak to him; we'll be playing the recording to him.'

'Oh . . . fine. My dear Louis, I wish you strength. You have the resources within you. And you got twenty out of twenty on your last test; you can be proud of yourself.'

Aside from me: Madame Ernest's encouragement is a bit crap, isn't it? She sounds like Master Yoda on a bad day.

'Thank you, Madame Ernest. I'm sure Louis will be very touched. But . . . I have a favour to ask you. For Louis and for all the other sick children around the world. I'd be grateful if you would agree.'

'I'll be delighted to help you if I can.'

'Good. So I'll explain. This is a bit awkward, so please don't be angry with me. There's a new social network challenge, called the boob challenge. It's for a good cause. It involves touching the breasts of different women to raise money for research into deep comas.'

'You're joking, I presume?'

'Not at all. I'm sure you're already seen those campaigns where celebrities pose bare-breasted to raise money for cancer research. . .'

'Yes, I think so . . .'

'Well, it's the same principle. The faces are pixelated, of course. It's all anonymous. For my contribution – to do my bit – my I've agreed to touch the breasts of everyone who's important to Louis. I'd very much like to touch your breasts, Madame Ernest.'

Aside, from me: Mum is almost sobbing as she says all that. She's amazing, my mother.

The scene ended in an extraordinary way. After the inevitable objections of my favourite maths teacher, Mum played Madame Ernest a video showing her touching the breasts of various women: my grandmother, of course, but also Charlotte, our favourite nurse, and Françoise, our cleaner. Then Madame Ernest finally said yes. Mum's hand moved towards her breast . . . and stopped a few centimetres from the finishing line. Such a pity.

Then, Mum straightened up, looked Madame Ernest in the eye and told her the whole truth about my notebook, and her crazy promise. She asked her if she still consented, now that she knew what it was all about. Of course, Madame Ernest said no, because it was her body, her choice, her right, blah, blah, blah. Obviously, what did Mum expect? OK, so it wasn't very cool to do a thing like that to Madame Ernest without telling her the real reason, but Mum had come up with such a brilliant idea!

Mum told me that it wasn't possible to touch the teacher's breasts without her informed consent. I'm not too sure what that means, but I felt really let down and thought that Mum had bottled out. Just then, she said, 'Don't be disappointed; I don't want you to think that I bottled out,' and I said to myself, OMG, now she can read my mind – that's the last straw (as Grandma would say). Mum gave me a bit of lecture explaining that this sort of thing wasn't acceptable, that she understood schoolboy fantasies, but touching a person's breasts without their consent was sexual abuse, and that what she had experienced was exactly what would have happened to me had I tried to touch Madame Ernest's breasts myself: I'd have been met with downright refusal, and a good thing too. I imagined Madame Ernest slapping my face or sending me to see the head, and I told myself that my mother was probably right. Mum ended up laughing and saying no wonder I fantasized about that teacher, she really was very pretty, but she was certain that, very soon, I'd be able to touch the breasts of lots of girls with their informed consent. And I tried not to think anything because I suspected that Mum could read my mind.

Then Mum and Grandma told me they wandered along the school corridors in search of Madame Grospiron, the English teacher I hate.

Having identified her, they snuck into her classroom, Grandma turned on the camera and then the light, and Mum stripped off in front of the table of irregular verbs. They laughed themselves silly and then found themselves face to face with the head teacher as they came out of the classroom. Mum was still hysterical, she told me. 'You should have seen his face ...' Then Mum played the sympathy card, saying she had to pick up her son Louis's exercise book. 'As you know, Monsieur Farès ...' Monsieur Farès melted and offered his sincere condolences. No one found that funny, and Mum told him I was alive, and that ruined the mood. Mum didn't laugh after that. She told me I had to be strong, that she still believed I could do it, that she loved me more than anything in the world and she missed me so much.

I don't recognize my mother. It's her, of course, but she's more open, cheerful and relaxed, and funnier. And she's also more sincere and more affectionate.

She's my mother, only better.

Excerpt from the Book of Wonders

I dare!!!
- *Touch Madame Ernest's boobs!*
- *Get into a taxi and yell, 'Follow that car!'*
- *Strip off in Madame Grospiron's class*

12

17 Days

CHARLOTTE FOREVER

When I left Louis's room after telling him, with much forced laughter, about the lewd antics of his mother and grandmother at the Paul Éluard High School, I was exhausted.

I needed to sit down, right there in the corridor, on the fourth floor. Just for a moment. That morning, I'd become aware of a detail which, as the day went by, had taken on a growing importance in my mind. Louis had seen almost nothing of the month of January 2017. He'd spent it in this room – room 405 – the decor of which made me feel ill.

I was sick of the sight of that window that afforded nothing but a dismal vista of geometric concrete blocks overlooking a greyish boulevard. Sick, too, of the green lino floor, of those walls, where stickers of laughing birds, weird spaceships and delicate flowers were supposed to distract from the suffocating smell of disinfectant. I'd had enough of the forced poetry, the feigned cheerfulness with which I filled the room, those smiling photos that contrasted painfully with the cries and moans that could sometimes be heard coming from the other end of the corridor. I'd had enough of all those tubes preventing me from touching my beautiful son. And I couldn't bear the thought that Louis might never see the spring again.

I found all these thoughts agonizing. Most of the time, I managed to keep them at bay, but the closer we were to 18 February – in other words, one month to the day from Dr Beaugrand's grim ultimatum – the heavier my sense of dread. Louis had to wake up now. Later would be too late. The crushing coldness of his absence would gradually kill me. I would not survive the arrival of a spring without him. Spring would be my physical and emotional limit.

Slumped in that uncomfortable hospital chair, lost in my thoughts, I'd adopted a position that, at first sight, looked like one of despair. My bowed head was cupped in my palms, and my fingers were making slow circular movements over my scalp. I gave myself a massage to stop myself from sinking into hopelessness. This was only the beginning of February. I had seventeen days left to rouse my son; I had to keep going.

I hadn't heard Charlotte approach and I jumped when she softly broke into my thoughts.

'Are you all right?'

'You gave me a fright . . . Yes, thank you, Charlotte, everything's fine. Feeling a bit down, that's all.'

'I'm off duty now; would you like me to give you a ride home? I believe you live near the Saint-Martin canal – it's on my way.'

'Thank you, that's very kind, but I don't want to trouble you. I'll walk – the fresh air will do me good.'

'If you want fresh air, you'll get plenty with me. I'm on a scooter. Come on, I'll give you a lift, and I won't take no for an answer.'

I didn't say yes, but I followed her out, anyway.

I'd realized a few days earlier that I'd developed a fondness for this young woman. Unlike some of her colleagues, she had always been very considerate with Louis, extremely respectful. Whereas some of the others had no hesitation in continuing their private conversations in front of my son, as if he wasn't there or was invisible, Charlotte spoke to him. Whereas others spoke to him as if he had learning difficulties, using honeyed tones and baby language, Charlotte described to him what she was doing, precisely and in a normal voice.

Charlotte did a difficult job, always with a smile. There was something luminous about her fair hair and radiant complexion, a hint of sunshine in her azure gaze. She had a huge, almost fierce joie de vivre that was infectious. All five foot one of her was impressive, with her self-assurance, composure and kindness. She was brave, and never complained in front of the patients or their families. I had started to look up to her, in a way. In any case, I respected her for what she was, what she exuded, what she did. And yet she must have had her own problems too. A leaky pipe to deal with, an overdraft to pay off, a cold she couldn't shake off, a boyfriend who wasn't phoning back, her scooter breaking down.

I had a sudden impulse to get to know her. I don't know why. Yes, I do know why. Because she appeared to love my son. 'Love' is perhaps a bit strong; over the years, she must have developed a thick skin to stop herself from crumbling in the face of all that human suffering, but she wasn't indifferent to this adolescent and his slightly wacky mother and grandmother.

What was her story? How had she decided to become a nurse? Where did she live? How old was she? Did she have children? Was she married? Did she have a dog, a cat, a hamster?

When we were outside my place, I found myself starting a conversation:

'Would you like to come up for a minute?'

'That's kind of you, but I wouldn't like to . . . and, in any case, I can't . . .'

'You know I'm asking you in because I want to. But, don't worry, I'm not hitting on you!' I added that last bit with a laugh, because I saw her hesitate and it occurred to me that my invitation – and especially the way I'd phrased it – might have sounded ambiguous.

She laughed too and replied that she hadn't imagined any such innuendo, but she really couldn't. After a pause, she finally said, 'To tell you the truth, I'm having a little party at my place tonight for my birthday – it was two days ago – and, if you'd like to come, you'd be welcome.'

'Thank you for the invitation, Charlotte – I'm deeply touched. Truly. But don't feel you have to ask me, and don't take your work home. You already put in so much effort at the hospital. No need to lumber yourself with your patients' depressed mothers . . . Happy birthday, all the same!'

'Thank you . . . You know I'm asking you because I want to. But, don't worry, I'm not hitting on you!'

We laughed again, and Charlotte insisted, assuring me that it would do me good and saying her place was just around the corner. She'd known that, like her, I lived close to the Saint-Martin canal, as did probably more than a hundred thousand Parisians, but she hadn't realized we were almost neighbours. She gave me her address, which turned out to be three streets away. If I felt bored or out of place, I could leave at any time; it would be a simple little dinner with friends, buffet style, people would be dropping in all evening. Then she added, with that typical twinkle in her eye, 'Let your hair down, it'll do you good – and I'd love you to come!'

I said yes. She said something like, 'Great, so see you around eight,' and I watched her slight form ride off on her scooter.

Shit – why had I accepted? What the hell was I going to be able to talk to all those strangers about? I looked at myself in my bedroom mirror and felt a surge of panic. This would be the first time I'd gone out since Louis's accident. I began inspecting myself by rolling up my trousers. I rolled them down again immediately, realizing with horror that my legs were more like those of Chewbacca than Miss World. My grey roots were beginning to show. At Hégémonie, I'd have been pelted with stones – or at least rotten tomatoes.

What time was it? Four fifteen. I had three and three-quarter hours to do something about it and make myself presentable. I started to thank the god of beauty salons that I lived in Paris and not in one of those small towns where everything closes at six. I still had time to get my legs waxed, buy some flowers to thank Charlotte, get my hair done and camouflage my wrinkles beneath one of the foundations that had been gathering dust in my cupboard for a month.

I grabbed my jacket and raced out. I'd left my mother a Post-it that would give her the shock of her life. I'd written, soberly but in a flurry of excitement, *Don't cook for me tonight – I'm going out.*

13

17 Days

A FILTHY OLD DIVE

A little party, Charlotte had said. Ha ha. The apartment was tiny and crammed.

It felt like the Hégémonie Christmas bash, the kind of party where anyone would think the guests had all fasted for three months ... All I ever managed to grab were three ham canapés, being too well brought up to push and shove. Well, at Charlotte's, you had to battle your way through to get anywhere near the buffet or the drinks.

Charlotte welcomed me, all smiles, and invited me in, thanking me for the flowers and gratifying me with a 'Wow – you look gorgeous!' which thrilled me. I'd chosen a simple but striking outfit: slim jeans, white semi-sheer blouse, statement blue heels. I returned the compliment. Charlotte looked stunning. Of course, I recognized her, but her evening look was totally different from the white coat, Crocs and light make-up that I was used to seeing. Perched on platform sandals that flattered her tanned legs and made her a good four

111

inches taller, she twirled in her black dress, bestowing her infectious zest for life on each guest. Given that there must have been fifty people, it didn't take me long to work out that my quota of Charlotte during the party would be very limited.

I'd been there for nearly twenty minutes and I still hadn't entered into conversation with anyone. I was the oldest guest there. Charlotte must have been ten years younger than me. I hadn't articulated it so clearly to myself at the hospital, but now that I was seeing her in her home surroundings, it was obvious. What the hell was I doing there? As the minutes went by, I felt more and more out of place. I was different from this crowd of young singles, who were carefree, laughing, drinking, smoking. And I envied them. I wanted to be like them, pull the wool over their eyes and make them believe I fitted in. I usually found water-cooler conversations so easy, but I'd lost that ability to feign interest in things that bored me, to respond with nods or 'Oh, wonderful . . . Oh, that was lucky . . . Wow, that's amazing . . .' to the wittering of a vague acquaintance telling me about their holiday in Nepal. These past weeks had numbed my socialization synapses. It hadn't dawned on me because I hadn't found myself in a situation like this since slamming the door of Hégémonie. I was about to leave, when I heard a man addressing me.

'It's unbelievable; these kids would do anything for a

few drops of alcohol. Can I offer you something, mademoiselle? If I manage to squeeze through, that is . . .'

He had a warm, husky voice, almost cracked. Very masculine. I turned around, a typical reply-that-takes-the-wind-out-of-the-sails-of-don-juans-who-talk-like-in-a-novel on the tip of my tongue: 'No, thank . . .' And stopped mid-sentence.

The guy was good looking. Charming. Not what I had been expecting. Forty, or a little more – it didn't matter – in any case, a lot older than the average age of the other guests. Tall, fairly classic features and a muscular physique that was visible through his loose, long-sleeved grey sweatshirt. A thin, well-kempt beard, longish curly black hair, which he'd smoothed behind his ears but which I could immediately tell he had trouble taming. Of Mediterranean origin, most likely, both coarse and sophisticated at the same time. Very dark, almost black eyes, with a steely glint, despite his smile – because he was smiling at me, waiting for my answer. I was standing rooted to the spot, probably looking a little gormless, and then a girl carrying several beers bumped into me. Crash. Beer spilt all over the floor. I desperately clutched at the person next to me. Missed. Slipped. Beer all over my white blouse. Humiliation.

The young woman apologized profusely, repeatedly calling me *madame*. Further humiliation. My handsome stranger had said *mademoiselle*, that was my consolation prize. Shit – my blouse. All I needed was a beer-soaked wet T-shirt competition ... I told the girl it didn't matter – 'Honestly, I assure you –' and my knight in shining armour held out his hands and helped me up. I was surprised by the contrast between his firm, vigorous grip, completely in keeping with his slightly gruff image, and his unusually long fingers. A man's hands are the first thing I look at – after his eyes and buttocks, of course. As for his bum, I hadn't managed to catch a glimpse of it yet, but his eyes and hands fulfilled their promise.

'I'm so sorry; it's all my fault ... If I hadn't distracted you–'

'Don't worry; it's nothing – and, besides, I love the smell of beer on my body.'

Jesus, Thelma, what kind of stupid joke is that? Can't you think of anything better?

'That's lucky. I also love the smell of beer on your body.'

The guy had a sense of humour. He was on a roll.

'Let's go back to where we left off, shall we? Allow me to offer you that drink I promised ...'

Where the hell did this guy, who looked like an action-movie hero and spoke like an educated actor, come from? Impossible to remain indifferent, in any case. I have to admit, I felt an immediate, almost animal attraction towards this stranger. It was inexplicable, disconcerting. Fucking pheromones.

I was going to say yes to the drink, but I stopped myself. I thought of Louis. I hadn't thought of Louis for twenty minutes. What was I doing? Forgetting my son? What right did I have to flaunt my alcohol-soaked breasts in front of a beau? A yawning abyss of guilt opened up and began to suck me in, punishing me for being capable of thinking lewd thoughts while my son was in a coma. My blouse was starting to reek like a filthy old dive. I found myself pathetic. I had to leave, right away.

'No, thank you, honestly. I have to go. In any case, I'm not presentable.'

'I assure you that you are much more than presentable. I insist. Let me get you that drink, then you can leave.'

'I'm sorry. Have a lovely evening.'

I grabbed my coat and went, without even saying goodbye to Charlotte, who was on the balcony, chatting with a young man and chain-smoking. She'd missed the unfortunate beer episode. Good; at least I'd preserve a shred of dignity in her eyes.

What an idiot I'd been to accept. I wasn't ready, I should have known. But I was so desperate to believe that my life could return to normal again. That I could return to normal. I'd been so wrong.

I was only five minutes away from home, but I needed to walk. For a long time. I couldn't go back so early;

Mum would bombard me with questions. She'd been even more excited than me at the thought of my going out. When I'd got back from the beautician's, she'd fussed over me endlessly, reminding me how wonderful I was, saying I was allowed to carry on living, to be happy. I had almost let myself be persuaded, but I'd come to realize a little belatedly that my sole priority, my love, my burden, my pain, my joy, my hope was still Louis.

Alone in the street, I walked beside the Saint-Martin canal, which my son had so loved. Tears filled my eyes when I noticed that I was thinking of him in the past tense. I held them back, just on the brink. The Saint-Martin canal that my son so *loves*. Louis isn't dead, Thelma. Louis is going to live.

The weather was mild for early February. I kept my coat open to dry my blouse, which gave off a very unpleasant odour. I'd gone from smelling like a filthy old dive to smelling like a club at around four in the morning.

I thought about my knight in shining armour. In the end, I'd learned nothing about him, but I could still feel the imprint of his hands on mine. I bit my lower lip, punishing myself for such inappropriate thoughts.

I sat down on a bench and gazed at the surface of the canal, wondering what it must feel like to drown: was it a painful death? Was it slow? Was it bearable? Dying seemed so easy. Why did we feel this profound need to live at all costs? Why was this damned instinct, this compulsion to hang on, so powerful? It would have been easier to let go. I could have leaned so far forwards that I'd have toppled in and sunk into the water of the muddy canal. No one would have seen me if I'd gone about it properly. But I couldn't let go, I knew. I was in purgatory, condemned to live.

I drew in the night air hungrily, with desperation, as if it were compressed oxygen from a cylinder in a hospital room.

14

16 Days

ONE, TWO . . .

The day after Charlotte's party, my mother questioned me non-stop, and she quickly sensed I was being evasive. I tried to make up some story or other, but I remembered that Mum knew Charlotte as well as I did, so she wouldn't have any trouble finding out that I left the party very early. Better to head her off with some woolly explanation: I didn't stay long because I wasn't feeling too good, probably something I'd eaten at lunchtime, or tiredness. I went out for some air, for a stroll through the city. Yes, of course everything's fine, Mother. She wasn't fooled – she never is – but she left me in peace. She said that Louis's little notebook was doing me good, was doing us all good. Maybe I could attack the next challenge; it would take my mind off things.

She was right. I had sixteen short days left and Louis was still showing no sign of waking up. The electro-encephalograms remained hopelessly unchanged, still as anarchic. I had asked if it was possible that moments of wakefulness, his brain's real activity, had been missed.

I was told that, with a coma, anything was possible, but that concern was growing as time went by.

Before opening my son's notebook, I held it close and sniffed it. It still gave off a few fleeting whiffs of Louis. At the hospital, Louis's only scent was that of the products they used to wash him. How much longer would these remnants of my son last? Time caused smells to fade, images to blur. I needed to look at photos to stop his eyes and his smile from being erased, keep them alive, not allow them to sink into the recesses of a memory that was becoming hazy much too quickly.

I stroked the cover of Louis's Book of Wonders. I flicked past the page about stripping naked in the English teacher's class and couldn't help smiling. Then I closed my eyes and turned the page. I opened only one eye, dreading what lay in store for me, prolonging the little pleasure that would also be short-lived. The number of pages Louis had filled was limited; he planned to live and add to it gradually. But Louis hadn't had enough time. Reading this new page, at first, I howled inwardly – 'Oh no, not that!' – then I gave a sort of nervous laugh that spoke volumes. As a matter of fact, I'd been expecting to find something to do with football in the notebook, I'd even been surprised that Louis's beloved sport wasn't the very first entry. For sure, the cover was plastered with football images, visual warnings that had prepared me mentally. Despite this expectation, the sentence was harsh, unfolding in his rounded hand-writing on the page which mocked me endlessly. I called my mother in and held out Louis's notebook. She burst out laughing, gratifying me with a 'Well, he's certainly putting you through your paces!'

There, in front of me, the treacherous football crime scene lay spread out with an exuberant defiance:

Football football football ☺ ☺ ☺

– Do an intensive course with Edgar, yes! (and Isa . . .)

So, who was this Edgar? His soccer coach, most likely. I vaguely remembered Louis mentioning that name . . . but I never listened properly when he was talking about football. On the other hand, what the hell was the mysterious Isa – this was the second time her name had appeared – doing in the midst of this nightmare?

Once over the shock, I wondered whether I could find a way of sidestepping this dream. I didn't mean to avoid honouring my promise – I'd do as instructed – but I could still try to make my own alternative interpretation of what he'd written. After all, Louis spoke of an intensive course, without specifying the content. Perhaps I could find someone called Edgar and a girl called Isabelle and ask them to play a football video game intensively for a few days, and that way fulfil the challenge while staying nice and snug at home?

I must confess that I've always hated football. I've never understood through what obscure genetic process my aversion could have mutated into a passion in my offspring. I don't recall whether Louis's father was particularly fascinated by the game either. No, this was something he had developed all by himself, no doubt encouraged by the global brands that spend millions on transforming morons with a limited vocabulary into intergalactic stars, and a completely ordinary sport into a top attraction. Of course, not everyone should be tarred with the same brush, not all the players are total idiots, but, even so, how has it become acceptable in our society for a footballer to earn ten thousand times more than a nurse, a teacher or a scientific researcher – real-life people, doing useful jobs? That is beyond me.

In my case, it's not just a question of football. I dislike sport in general. I did a bit of dance between the ages of ten and thirteen with relative enthusiasm, although I always contrived to miss the end-of-year show. At secondary school, I was one of the girls who had a stomach ache, who had her period, a persistent headache, a twisted ankle . . . any excuse to get out of gym classes.

But, if Louis were conscious, how would he react to my shameless perversion of his dream, which was actually so simple to put into practice?

Are you kidding, Mum? Is that how you expect to motivate me, by making up lies and not even attempting to take an interest in the thing I'm passionate about? You've never been interested, anyway . . .

But I hate football, as you well know . . .

So, I'm not worth a little physical effort, is that it? If only you knew what I'd give to be in your shoes!

If only you knew how much I wish you could be in my shoes. I'd give my right arm to be able to change places with you, my darling.

After this dithering and my imaginary conversation with Louis, I had to face the facts. I couldn't back out. I resolved to seek out this man, Edgar. It was Thursday, 2 February, the half-term holiday would begin in two days' time – maybe there were courses being organized. Football courses for beginner oldies? Some hope! I was going to have to persuade the coach to allow me to take part in one of his sessions for pimply youths. They'd think I was crazy, but I was beginning to get used to that.

I flicked through the admin file, and looked in the section headed *Louis*: school lunch bills, medical certificates and subscriptions of all kinds. Registration for his guitar lessons (he gave up after three months), his table-tennis course (I warned him he wouldn't like it, but he wouldn't listen, and he hated it), registration for football, football, football. From the age of six. In the early years, I had to get up at five o'clock in the morning on a miserable June day to go and queue to sign him up. The leisure-centre staff didn't arrive until nine, but I had to stand there from dawn, surrounded by parents ready to do anything to get their brat on to the course for their favourite sport, glaring daggers at anyone who stepped over the imaginary line they'd drawn to indicate that they were first in the queue. This year, I'd managed to duck out of that chore; Louis was big now, and I'd sent him to do his own queuing – well, not completely . . . in the company of two of his footie friends and the mother of one of them. He'd waited and signed himself up. Since the beginning of the school year, in September, he'd been going to training sessions and coming home on his own, and I'd managed to wriggle out of going to watch any tournaments or matches. I was very proud of the success of my avoidance strategy and boasted about it around the coffee machine at Hégémonie, declaring myself a disgraceful mother and laughing about it. At the time, I sincerely thought that it meant I was a woman who successfully juggled being a mother and working.

I felt a pang as I realized the extent to which I'd completely dismissed this passion of Louis's, the extent to which I'd treated it as a permanent joke, and how upset he must have been at my excuses. Parental approval and interest are so important. In months, I hadn't devoted a single minute of my precious time to football. Football wouldn't suffer, I said to myself. Football hadn't suffered, of that I could be sure, but what about Louis? Wasn't this wholesale rejection of my son's passion the same as my mother's rejection of the normal capitalist world I so wanted to be part of, a stance that had exasperated me when I was a teenager? How come I had replicated my mother's behaviour so automatically? Louis had appeared to deal with it . . . of course, what else could he do? But what would it have cost me to show a little interest? A few hours standing around on the sidelines, cheering him on, giving him a little encouragement; a few smiles in my eyes, in his. That, too, I had missed out on, and I deeply regretted it.

I was finding it increasingly hard to cope with what I was learning about myself, about my past behaviour. I wanted to change my life completely, change everything and make it all different, make it all better. I'd had a long conversation with Mum about it, the previous day. Or rather, Mum had launched into one of her typical diatribes:

'You can't throw the baby out with the bathwater,' she'd lectured. 'You're not a perfect mother, you're not a perfect woman, you're not a perfect daughter – that I can assure you . . . but you do what you can. Everyone manages as best they can, and it's not a question of perfect mothers and hopeless mothers, pussycat. I've seen you with Louis, thousands of times. In his eyes, you're the perfect mother, because you're his mother. Don't ever doubt that. If Louis is what he is today – and it's not because he's my grandson, but objectively – he's a delightful boy, bright, sensitive and kind ... well, if that's what he's like now, it's thanks to you. You're the one who's raised that kid, and you can be proud of him. No, don't say anything. I can see you shaking your head and you're likely to come out with something stupid. You can be proud of yourself. *I'm* proud of you.'

My mother has a knack for making me blubber with her great monologues, which she always delivers just when I need them most. Being there and saying the right thing is also part of being a mother.

I grabbed my phone and called the community centre. Yes, there would indeed be courses during the holidays. No, none for adults. For under- and over-thirteens courses, I should contact Edgar directly. His training sessions were on Wednesday afternoons and Friday evenings.

'Thank you, madame, I understand. I'll go and see Edgar and sign up.'

15

15 to 10 Days

EDGAR

'OK, you can put the balls down and we'll all go for something to drink . . . No shoving!'

Shit, I was in agony. My lungs were on fire, and every muscle in my body hurt like hell. I'd even discovered some I didn't know I had. How was it possible to feel pain between my ribs and in my biceps, from playing football? When I'd embarked on this, I'd been expecting some discomfort, but I never thought I'd have aches and pains from head to foot. I was paying the price for my lack of exercise over the past twenty-five years. If I hadn't promised Louis, I'd have long since given up these torture sessions. This was day three, I still had another day to get through. I was tempted to carve little lines on a tree, like a prisoner counting the days until freedom.

Edgar came over and asked me if everything was all right. I could have replied curtly, of course, that I'd never felt so good in all my life, that I'd always dreamt of sprawling in the mud with a bunch of sweaty prepubescents, but I refrained. I tossed my hair back into place, saying, 'Yes, yes, everything's fine – a bit tired, that's all.' Something of an understatement, for someone whose muscles and respiratory system had turned to jelly.

Edgar. If there was one positive thing about this entire experience, it was meeting Edgar. The guy was incredible. I kept looking for a flaw, but couldn't find one. What I felt was strange, new. I cursed him all day long – his exercises, his natural authority, which shut up the most rebellious of my pre-teen co-detainees – and, at the same time, I admired him. I admired him for his simplicity, his genuineness, his almost animal strength, and for the vulnerabilities I'd sensed. I felt as if I'd known him forever.

When I'd turned up at the Friday evening training session to ask for details of the courses on offer and to sign up – my heart filled with dread – I'd had to wait in a small room next to the community-centre sports ground, where I'd sipped a coffee that was too sweet as I honed my strategy.

I planned to come clean with Edgar, and tell him the truth about my project. I anticipated his likely reluctance. I'd brought Louis's hospitalization certificate as proof, so he wouldn't suspect me of being a predatory paedophile. I was prepared for every possible reaction. And I was ready to bribe him, if necessary.

I waited for the famous Edgar, and imagined him to be like Monsieur Ducros, my P.E. teacher when I was fourteen, whom we nicknamed 'Little Ninja' because he was both tiny and paunchy, but astonishingly agile. Monsieur Ducros gave us mind-blowing gymnastics demonstrations, transforming himself into a bouncing ball of energy, contrary to expectations. To look at him, no one would have bet a cent on his ability to teach any kind of sports discipline.

I was absorbed in my memories, staring into space, when I saw the stranger I'd met at Charlotte's little party walk into the room. My nostrils quivered, recalling the smell of dried beer that had clung to me during the long hours I'd wandered along the towpath of the Saint-Martin canal. I neither wanted to relive the feelings of that disastrous and painful evening, nor to flirt, even if my knight was still as attractive. I looked away and devoured the fascinating activities brochure over and over.

'Hello. We've already met, haven't we? You are . . . We met at my sister's birthday party.'

'Hello. I . . . Yes, I remember . . . Hello – sorry, I already said that . . . You're Charlotte's brother? I had no idea she had an older brother . . . I mean . . .'

'. . . That I look older than her? That I was out of place among all those young people at her apartment? No hard feelings; I thought so, too, and I was pleasantly surprised to meet you that night . . . I mean . . .'

'. . . That I looked older than the average age, there? That I was out of place, too? I agree, and I think that makes us quits.'

Jesus, what an idiot . . . Incapable of putting a coherent sentence together, and punctuating my babbling with silly little giggles . . . So, I'd made a fool of myself two days earlier in front of the brother of pretty Charlotte, who was as blonde as he was dark. I'd never have guessed they were related. I was going to try to run away, once again, but he wouldn't let me.

'I'm very glad to see you again; you left so abruptly the other evening, we didn't even have a chance to introduce ourselves.'

'I'm sorry . . . I'm Thelma.'

I held out my hand. He took it and held on to it for a few seconds longer than was necessary.

'I know who you are. I described you to my sister after the party and she . . . explained the situation. I'm very sorry about your son, Thelma, truly. Especially because I'm very fond of him.'

'I beg your pardon? Who are you very fond of?'

'Your son, Louis. When my sister told me . . . I realized that . . . My sister and I rarely talk about our work. She has a demanding job in the intensive-care unit, so, when we're together, we talk about everything except her day-to-day work at the hospital. In any case, she never talks about her patients, and I never talk to her about my kids . . . Well, not really mine – the ones I coach. It's a small world. Paris is a village, and it so happens that, at the moment, my sister's looking after one of my pupils: your son, Louis. I'm Edgar. Delighted to meet you, Thelma.'

Oh my God. Oh my God. Oh my God. Oh my God (as my son would say). The guy I'd made an idiot of myself in front of was Charlotte's brother and Louis's football coach. I could never, ever have guessed, especially because he looked neither like Sophie Davant nor Monsieur Ducros, the Little Ninja.

We sat down for a moment, and I calmly told him the reason why I was there. He was moved by my story, that was obvious. He told me that he'd accept me on one of his four-day half-term courses, and annoyed me a little by saying he'd rather put me with the eight-to-twelve-year-olds. The thirteen-to-sixteens were fairly rough, and I might get hurt, which wasn't the aim. What's more, he had fully grasped the urgency of my situation, and the course for the younger ones started first. Sunday, actually. He added that, given the circumstances, I could do just one or two days, but I insisted on doing all four. It's what Louis would have done, so that's what I had to do. I would just have to get a move on with the following challenges – hoping that they didn't include any more long courses. Edgar smiled when I let slip the word 'challenges'. Then he gave me his phone number and asked for mine, so he could let me know if the course was cancelled at the last minute – officially.

The next morning, I told Louis what I was going to

do. Charlotte mentioned that her brother was a tough coach and that I'd better get myself into shape beforehand, otherwise I'd find it hard going. Naturally, I ignored her advice. I spent the Saturday afternoon preparing myself physically in my own way: I had to find an outfit that wouldn't make me look like a shapeless sack in football boots. I also attempted to learn about football by watching two matches . . . which confirmed my lack of interest in the game – both times, I fell asleep at half-time.

*

On day one of the course, I was the centre of attention. Eleven hyped-up kids stared at me, laughing their heads off at the idea that I'd be training with them. Edgar hadn't told them that I was Louis's mother, because most of them knew him, and he didn't want that to interfere with the training. Nor did he want to have to justify my presence to the parents, who might have asked if they too could take part in the course . . . So Edgar introduced me as a journalist doing an article on football. That's why I'd always be wearing a helmet with a little camera filming my face, to capture my expressions. Everyone should treat me normally, with respect – 'Don't forget she's an adult' – but should see me as just another student. No preferential treatment; everyone would do the same exercises, with the same discipline; there would be no exceptions. For a second, I saw his eyes burn with that sports teacher's fire, and I was reminded of Monsieur Ducros, the Little Ninja, and the glint he aimed at deserters – which I was – to warn them of zero tolerance. I gave him a knowing smile, which, for me, meant, *We've understood each other: I'm not going to do exactly as these children do; I have the right to sit out, if I want* . . . But he didn't return my smile: he was serious. I realized I was up shit creek.

I was among nine boys and two girls. I immediately wondered whether one of the girls was the Isa that Louis mentioned in his precious notebook, but these two were called Dora and Zara – a comic-strip heroine and a clothing brand – so no luck there, even though the pair of them were pretty and smiling. The boys had various wacky names, typical of this generation of parents, who liked to show their creativity by giving their offspring unusual monikers. So I was surrounded by Miles, Esteban, Jean-Rachid, Artus, Leonardo, Amadou, Gabor, Aly-with-a-*y* and Milou.

Edgar divided us into four groups and we put on fluorescent-yellow T-shirts. I was with Milou and Jean-Rachid, whom the others just called Rachid. They seemed super chuffed to be with me, and Milou even called me 'Miss' at one point. That made Rachid burst out laughing and he retorted that I wasn't a teacher, that was obvious. I asked him what made him think that, and he replied that I didn't appear to be very fond of children. I stopped the camera. I wanted him to explain, but Edgar saw us and ordered us to get moving. I soon understood what Rachid had meant, and how distant and superior I must have seemed to them. Since the start of the morning, I'd been much more focused on the camera than on the moment. I got a grip on myself and smiled at Rachid, telling him I'd show him, and that I'd give him a hard time with my vast footballing experience. He laughed, gave me a high five and said, 'Let's go.'

And go we did. Jesus, we'd been going at it for three days. Those kids were tireless. I tried various ruses to get out of some of the sessions, including my classic twisted ankle. Edgar asked the kids to vote to decide whether or not I'd twisted my ankle, and they all voted no. I tried the urgent phone-call tactic, and Milou declared that my phone hadn't rung. I tried to bribe a child with a lot of sweets, and that worked: Dora was happy to pretend to feel unwell, and I offered to look after her. Edgar had no choice but to accept.

I spent a couple of delightful hours with young Dora. We played 'Guess who I'm thinking of', 'I dare you', 'Truth or dare', and she told me jokes that kids her age love – Dora had just turned twelve – and I laughed as I hadn't laughed for years. Laughing with her in those changing rooms that reeked of sweat and dirty socks, I began to feel nauseous. At first, it was vague, and then it became more insistent, oppressive.

This girl's energy and magnetic cheerfulness contrasted so painfully with my isolation, my solitude. The echo of the void resounded deep inside me. Dora's laugh was like a mirror in which all I could see was a black hole. I'd been absent from my own life for a very long time – since well before Louis's accident.

I tried to concentrate on Dora again – her jokes, her blond curls, her bubbly personality – but I couldn't. A door had just opened and I wasn't able to stem the stream of images that suddenly came flooding over me. I realized just how precious moments of complicity with a child could be, how I hadn't taken enough time to share such moments with Louis, how egotistical I'd been, self-centred, obsessed with my work. How I'd neglected the most important things. The tears came, silent tears. How long was it since I'd spent two hours, two little hours, alone with my son? Shame mingled with my tears, coloured my words. I felt paralysed by their weight. Heavy words, burdened with the terrible truth: you've been a bad mother, Thelma. You should have done so much more, you should have done so much better.

I tried to hide my emotion by pretending I had a speck of dust in my eye, but, to my great surprise, Dora gave me a hug. I'd just made myself look ridiculous, on top of the shame. And yet, in the skinny arms of this little girl, something inside me gave way. She started to speak to me, to comfort me the way a parent soothes a child in the middle of the night. The world was upside down.

Then she said a few words that were to change our lives forever, although neither of us knew it at the time.

16

15 to 10 Days

DORA

'Papa told me everything. I love Louis very much, too. That's why Papa let me come back to the changing room with you. You know he didn't believe you. He knows when I'm not feeling well, because I make a big fuss. I'm a rubbish actress and I hate people who lie. So does Papa. I think you needed to cry – it's not good to bottle all that up, it had to come out. Papa always says to me, "Isa, sweetheart, it's better to show your feelings and look stupid, rather than keep things inside you." I think he's right, and that's not because he's my father, OK? Oh, and, actually, I hate sweets. I know, it's weird – everyone likes sweets. I guess I'm just not like everyone else.'

I sat up and dried my tears. I was gobsmacked by this incredibly mature monologue. In a few sentences, this little girl had just revealed an amount of information that my brain was struggling to process:

1. She'd spoken of Edgar as *Papa*.
2. She knew Louis.
3. She'd referred to herself as *Isa*.

To recap: she was Edgar's daughter. That was clear. Once again, there was no visible family likeness. Now I knew the connection, I was able to detect a few resemblances between her and Charlotte – just about. Edgar stood out strikingly in this fair-haired family. I wondered what this child's mother must look like and I felt an irrational pang. I pictured her as very beautiful, very fair – as fair-haired as I was dark. I've always borne a grudge against blondes. They have some connection with envy, desire. Blondes represent a fantasy, for men and women alike. Brunettes are reality – wallpaper that blends into the surroundings. They only make waves when their hair is jet black. The brunette is in between, only revealing her true flavour when you really taste her. I've sometimes thought of bleaching my hair, but I've always given up the idea, full of lofty principles that made me narrow-minded. At the end of the day, perhaps I should have tried.

Another crucial nugget of information that she'd let slip: it sounded as if she was Louis's Isa. The one who'd made my heart skip a beat, from the first page of the precious notebook. I felt a huge sense of relief mixed with huge embarrassment. Relief at finally being able to put a face to the name of the girl I'd fantasized about hundreds of times over the past weeks. Above all, at being able to associate that name with a child's face. The Isa in the notebook could have been an adult in whom Louis had confided, who was important to him. I'd have died of jealousy. Louis was my child, and I couldn't bear the idea of another woman stealing his attention. I thanked the heavens – just the heavens; there was no divine being in my imagination – that this Isa was a child, a pre-teen; it didn't matter. Any-thing except another woman. So, a huge relief, but I also felt huge embarrassment at having made such an idiot of myself in front of her, revealing, one by one, the less admirable sides of my personality: I'd shown myself to be a cheat, always whingeing, a deserter, lazy, tearful. At least I hadn't pretended to be anything I wasn't.

At that precise moment, Edgar and the rest of the troop marched into the confined space of the changing rooms, raising the noise and smell levels. Some of the kids were chanting 'We are the champions!' and imi-tating the victory signs of their stadium idols, others snorted angrily and wore the expressions of would-be presidential candidates learning the fatal outcome of a bitterly contested election. Edgar laughed, rubbing the heads of the disappointed kids, finding the words to comfort them. A family trait, apparently. I stood up and headed for the adults' changing room. Before leaving, I wanted to thank Isa.

'Thank you, Isa . . . or Dora? What am I supposed to call you? I must say, I don't understand–'

'Both, captain. My name's Isadora. Like the dancer, Isadora Duncan. Mum was a dancer. Papa . . . Papa calls me Isa, and everyone else either calls me Dora or Isa, so it's up to you.'

I collected my sports holdall and slowly left the sports ground, taking the time to digest all this news.

I was exhausted.

As I walked through the gates, Edgar caught up with me and wouldn't let me go. Literally. He invited me to dinner at his place – their place. I protested, for form's sake, but then I very quickly accepted.

I entered their world. I wanted to.

*

Edgar and Isadora lived with Charlotte. It was their choice, and they made a happy household. Their apartment was where I had first met Edgar, but it felt very different without the extra fifty people in it. Although it was small, they each had their own room, their personal space.

'It's important for everyone, especially schoolgirls,' Edgar had joked, giving his daughter a knowing wink.

Charlotte was on night duty at the hospital that

evening, so it was just the three of us. Isadora took me into her den. Seeing the posters of footballers, I felt my legs turn to jelly. I had to lean against a wall to stop myself from crumpling. Her room was so similar to Louis's, it was disturbing. Now, I understood the bond between them, their shared passion – the attraction of those ecstatic victory gestures on glossy paper. The champions were jubilant, exuding extreme pride and elation. Visceral snapshots of fleeting joys, so enthralling. I didn't dare ask Isa about her relationship with Louis. She held out a scarf, signed by some obscure player. She teased me gently, wondering how it was possible not to have heard of Zlatan Ibrahimović. I replied, 'It's easy, you see . . .' then I handed back the precious scarf. With a solemn expression, she placed it in my hands like an offering, asking me to give it to Louis when he woke up. Because he was going to wake up, she just knew it. I hugged her and began to cry. She pushed me gently away, forcing herself to laugh, saying, 'Oh no, you're not going to start that again . . .' More role reversal. I thanked her, saying I was sure Louis would be thrilled with her gift. She thought so too.

We ate pizza, sitting on the floor. Edgar had put on the soundtrack from Jane Campion's *The Piano* as background music. I recognized it at once. An excellent choice – that was one of my favourite films, and the music was quite simply astounding. My mental portrait of Edgar was becoming clearer. Edgar was a man who easily managed to gain the respect of a whole group of adolescents, a man who showed such consideration for his daughter and had created with her a complicity based on mutual respect and teasing, a man capable of rolling in the mud in the morning and of being stirred by Michael Nyman's exquisite piano playing in the evening, a man with a generous smile and dark, sad eyes, a man who must enjoy great success with women, but who seemed oblivious of his powers of attraction. That week, I'd seen the mothers simpering when they came to pick up their children . . . and 'Edgar this,' and 'Edgar that'. I sensed in him a tumult of joys and sorrows. Isadora had spoken of her mother in the past tense. Who was he? What had he been through? I was increasingly intrigued. I was in turmoil, and I wanted to know more.

After only a few minutes, we were using the informal *tu*, and I'd begun to let go, to relax. Louis stayed in a corner of my mind, all the time. Everything brought me back to him. Allowing myself to eat with others was a big step for me. I told myself that these people were in my son's precious notebook, they were important to him, and that Louis had implicitly approved our friendship because it was he who'd pointed me in the direction of Isadora and Edgar. By staying, I was entering my son's world, in a way. I was aware that I was enjoying it a great deal.

At around ten o'clock, to my amazement, Isa announced it was her bedtime – whereas I used to have a nightly battle with Louis to get him to go to his room. She kissed us, and Edgar went to tuck her up.

I was left alone for a few moments. The contrast with my own living room was striking. My place was all designer chic, sterile, impersonal. But, here, the untidiness was part of the decor. Magazines lay on the floor, a few games too. The top of the solid wood sideboard was covered in dusty knick-knacks, but no one could blame those who lived there. I could see immediately that they had better things to do than dusting. They were busy living. Here, everything was vibrantly alive.

I got up and gathered my belongings.

'Thank you again, Edgar, it was really delicious.'

'Not true, of course. Industrial pizza, not a great cook . . . but it's kind of you to say so. But why are you on your feet? You look as if you're about to leave. That's out of the question. I won't let you give me the slip again.'

'I'm not giving you the slip, Edgar. I don't know whether you've noticed, but I'm spending my days with you, at the moment.'

'Again, not true. You're spending a lot of time nattering in the changing room . . . I'm joking. You know what I mean . . .'

A hesitation, a breath.

'I'd like you to stay.'

He came over to me and gently put my coat and bag down on the sofa. His hand brushed mine, or was it no accident? I felt a shiver run through my body.

I stayed.

Edgar offered me a herbal tea. I retorted that I wasn't an old lady yet, and that I'd rather he uncorked another bottle of wine. During the course of the evening, under the combined effect of the alcohol and the whispering, 'so as not to wake Isa', Edgar opened up. I didn't ask anything. He was the one who talked, spontaneously, freely. Several times, I said he didn't have to tell me anything, but he told me he wanted to. Needed to.

I learned their story. Heartbreakingly sad. As bleak as he and Isa were joyful.

3

Princes and Princesses

17

15 to 10 Days

IN VINO VERITAS

A few years ago, Isadora still had a mother. Edgar had met Madeleine when they were children. They had been madly in love.

*

In the 1980s, Edgar's father worked in a bank and his mother was a dance teacher. She had a little school in Paradise Street, in Marseille. You couldn't make it up. Dance was her whole life, which is why she chose the name Edgar for her son, after the Impressionist artist, Edgar Degas, who was famous for his beautiful ballerina paintings, prints of which adorned the walls of the school. Madeleine was one of her students. The best. The most beautiful, too. Madeleine dreamed of stardom, the Bolshoi, the Paris Opera. After his day at school or football training, Edgar always went to the dance school to wait for his mother. While doing his homework, his attention would wander, then he'd go and sit in a corner and watch the dance class, and draw. His mother was hugely proud of his talent. 'My Edgar will become a famous artist too,' she was forever saying.

Edgar drew the dancers. As the years went by, his pencil dwelt on the features of one girl in particular. Edgar drew Madeleine, but Madeleine didn't know it. At fourteen, Edgar finally plucked up the courage to take the first step. He gave Madeleine a portrait, immortalizing her precise movements, the perfection of her arabesque. She was deeply touched. From then on, Madeleine and Edgar became inseparable.

Madeleine loved Edgar's drawings. She encouraged him to persevere, to exhibit. While Edgar was a student at the Marseille School of Fine Arts, Madeleine auditioned, failed, picked herself up and failed again. After a few years of this, like many dancers, she opted for security, and began teaching at the family dance school. Madeleine was happy, her life revolved around her relationship with Edgar. He was beginning to gain a reputation, each one of his paintings selling for several thousand euros. He didn't sell many, so Madeleine's income brought a welcome stability to this family of artists.

Then, twelve years ago, Isadora came along. Their happiness lasted until Isadora started primary school. Then their world fell apart.

One September morning, Edgar's parents boarded flight MX484 for Havana. Forty years of marriage was something to celebrate. Family and friends chipped in to send the lovebirds on a second honeymoon. They'd always dreamt of going to Cuba. 'Retirement is the start of a new life,' joked Edgar's mother in her farewell speech to the dance school, which she'd handed over to Madeleine a few weeks earlier.

The plane never reached Cuba. The Atlantic would never yield any information. Every possible theory was put forward: human error, engine failure, terrorist attack . . . The black box was never found. It wasn't possible for the families of the 337 people who had perished to mourn. But, somehow, they had to start grieving.

Edgar threw himself into his work, but he found his paintings repetitive, depressing. The spark had gone. Madeleine provided for the household's needs single-handedly. They both protected Isadora as best they could. Madeleine spent more and more time at the dance studio, making it her duty to perpetuate the memory of the woman who'd given her everything: her passion, her school, her son. She seemed exhausted, unsurprisingly, given how hard she worked.

On 20 December 2011 – Edgar would remember the date for the rest of his days – at around six o'clock in the evening, when Isadora was still in her bath, Edgar received a phone call. La Timone Hospital. Madeleine had become unwell in the middle of a dance lesson. The ambulance had taken her to the hospital and they were going to run some tests. Probably exhaustion, they'd

149

said at the time. Edgar hurriedly dried Isadora and hurtled through Marseille's crowded streets at the wheel of his old grey Clio. His head was telling him that everything would be fine, ordered him to slow down and stop panicking, but his heart told him otherwise. His heart was pounding in his ribcage. It was always one step in front of his head.

The diagnosis fell like a ton of bricks, incomprehensible and yet perfectly clear. Edgar cursed his heart for having understood too much. Cancer of the intrahepatic bile ducts. Rare. Terrifying. Devastating. 'Metastasized, the chances of survival are around five per cent. We are very sorry, monsieur.'

For three months, Madeleine fought. She didn't give up. Three months is a long time. Three months is no time at all. A few hours before she died, Madeleine was still joking with her daughter. Her last thoughts were for her. She must never see me cry. She must remember me as a fighter. Women are able to fight if they are taught to when they are still little girls. I will teach her to fight, until my last breath.

*

Edgar broke off. I had listened to him fervently, without interrupting. As he unspooled the fragile thread of his life, Edgar was at the same time preoccupied and grave, while maintaining a salutary emotional distance.

150

Keeping well away from deep waters so as not to drown. He had such tremendous dignity.

I, on the other hand, was in a terrible state. A tear-stained face, sniffing loudly, soggy tissue. Edgar held out a fresh box. I asked him why he was telling me all this. He replied that it was necessary. That I couldn't really know him if I didn't know this about him. It was part of him, and always would be. I almost told him that it was a little presumptuous to think that I wanted to know him so intimately, but I refrained. That would have been very rude, but, most of all, completely untrue, because I absolutely did want to get close to him.

I took a deep breath and poured myself another glass of wine. So did he. Huddled on the sofa, under a patchwork quilt that Isadora had made with Charlotte, I was silent. He went on, smiling openly – this guy was incredible – saying that the rest of the story would be a lot less sad.

*

That year, Charlotte was due to finish her nursing studies. A few years earlier, she'd moved to a tiny apartment in the centre of Paris. Charlotte loved the capital, which isn't always the case for a girl from the south. She'd fallen crazily in love with the city and with one of its inhabitants. The affair didn't last, but her love for Paris remained unchanged. During those dark days of their lives, Charlotte put her studies on hold to go and help her brother and her niece. And to save herself. She spent six months with Isadora and Edgar, helping to heal their inner wounds. They healed hers in return. From then on, it was just the three of them. It would always be the three of them. They swore it. *It's the three of us for life, for life.* That was their motto. Etched in their flesh.

Then Charlotte had this brilliant idea. They would drop everything. They had no reason to stay in Marseille, and Charlotte needed to finish her nursing studies. They'd find an apartment in Paris that was big enough for the three of them. And they'd recreate what they had lost – a home.

Isadora loved the idea. Edgar could no longer bear to live in Marseille, wandering those streets that reminded him of his lost loved ones. He had to move on. For Isa's sake. For his own. For their sakes. Charlotte was amazing, there was no other word for it. The bond that united the three of them now was much stronger than that of a brother and sister.

Edgar sold the dance school. The money would enable him to get by for eighteen months, during which time he hoped to find the inspiration to paint once more, but he could no longer do it. Nothing is more volatile than creativity. His savings dwindled and Charlotte's salary as a nurse wasn't enough. So Edgar got a grip on himself. He applied for one of the various youth-leader jobs, created by the City of Paris in 2013 as part of their reform of the school timetable, reducing it to four and a half days a week. The work wasn't well paid and was only part time, so he also ran sports courses at leisure centres to supplement his income. He wasn't mad about football, he'd played it for a few years when he was a kid, but Edgar loved children. The youth-work qualification he'd obtained when he was sixteen would finally prove useful.

For over two years now, Edgar had been living again. Isadora was his daily ray of sunshine. But she, having been put in ballet shoes at the age of three by her mother, now refused to have anything to do with the world of dance, saying she preferred football. A shell, a necessary protective skin. Edgar no longer drew – that, too, was over. They'd turned a page.

Of course, the past was – and always would be – present, but now Edgar was looking to the future. And what he saw was beautiful.

*

While he talked, I cried relentlessly. Their story was devastating. Heartbreaking.

Isadora, Charlotte and Edgar were survivors. I understood now what made the three of them so radiant: their smiles were genuine.

It was such a powerful message of hope for me ... After every nightmare, a new day dawns. I'd been waiting for the dawn since Louis's accident, but I realized that I had to keep moving forward in the dark, that it was still possible to carve out a path, no matter how dense the blackness.

The second bottle of wine was empty. Once again, I asked Edgar why he'd told me all this. Nowadays, he said, he listened to his heart. It was the only thing he trusted. His heart had told him to talk to me, to tell me everything. To be able to open doors, you have to know what is concealed in the dark and not be afraid of it. Edgar knew that my doors would remain closed, that I wasn't yet ready to speak, and, in any case, he wasn't asking me to. I would talk later. Edgar's heart was never wrong. His heart had known, the first time he saw me. From the first moment, in that jam-packed apartment.

I was feeling increasingly uncomfortable. He was talking to me as if we were a couple. I said as much, and he answered that he was aware of it, of course, that it was obvious. I suddenly felt very hot. Other confused feelings mingled with my embarrassment. An inappropriate sense of elation. An intoxication hidden beneath layers of a cracked veneer.

I arrived home at around three o'clock in the morning. Unable to get to sleep, I went into the room where my mother slept. I leaned over her and whispered that I loved her.

Half asleep, she said, 'What are you doing here, pussycat?' and threw her soft bony arms around me.

It was exactly what I needed.

18

9 to 6 Days

RAINBOW COLOURS

The next stage of the precious notebook was to go to Budapest, and what Louis had concocted for me to do there was no cakewalk, as my mother put it.

The main challenge was to take part in a race called The Color Run, which claims to be 'where sport meets fun'. Mum did a Web search and made me watch a video that said it all: thousands of people in white T-shirts and protective goggles having clouds of coloured paint thrown in their faces for every kilometre they completed, ending up a total mess, naturally. I couldn't see the fun in that, but the runners looked happy.

'A bunch of drug addicts, probably . . .' Mum remarked, before learning that these masochistic urban communions had already attracted several million people around the globe.

I was starting to get stressed when I discovered that, beneath its festive appearance, this event was a half marathon, that Budapest was a very hilly city, and my body was still battered from the football ordeal. Since the Budapest race wouldn't be taking place until May, I'd have to create my own event. I suddenly had this pathetic vision of chucking coloured paints over myself and collapsing, exhausted, on a hilly street . . . Clearly, I was going to need help with throwing the paints and with my likely physical feebleness.

I asked Edgar to come with me. My mother – who never misses a trick – offered to come instead, sniggering with Charlotte in the hospital corridor.

'Don't be offended, Mum, but you're not exactly built like a tank, and I'm going to need physical support. I think Edgar's a much sounder option, that's all.'

I went in to see Louis, congratulated him on all his sporting ambitions, which were news to me, and explained to him that I was relying on Edgar to stop me having a heart attack on the Hungarian capital's famous Chain Bridge.

'Edgar's going to film me, and Granny Odette will show you the whole thing live, on the iPad. Grandma can also cheer me on – right, Grandma? – because I'll have the headphones and mic on all the time.'

'Yes, of course, pussycat,' she replied, a little too enthusiastically.

*

Edgar threw himself wholeheartedly into his mission and took care of all the preparations. He explained that the coloured paints could easily be found in Passage Brady, the 'little India' district of Paris, because throwing paint was an ancient Hindu tradition: during Holi, the spring equinox festival, crowds of Indians paraded through the streets spraying coloured water over one another. Westerners had simply adapted the concept, adding a sporting dimension. No, the simple corn starch with natural dyes wouldn't leave a stain on me, and no, we weren't going to get ourselves banged up by the Hungarian police ... 'It's all perfectly harmless, don't worry.'

When we arrived in Budapest, we dropped our luggage off at the apartment I'd rented, two bedrooms of course, and Edgar asked me to wait for a couple of hours before walking to meet him at the foot of the Buda Castle Funicular – he had 'a few details to sort out'.

Finally, I was ready to set off, bundled up in my white puffa jacket, and Edgar was waiting for me, camera at the ready. Very soon, I realized that this race would be a physical ordeal festooned with zany, poetic touches. Edgar had organized a little welcome committee every two kilometres, made up of assorted families, old ladies, students, shopkeepers and tourists amused by the spectacle I offered. My supporters had laid a white sheet on the ground next to where they stood, so as not to stain the pretty medieval streets. I'd stop for a few seconds, close my eyes, and set off again splattered with a new colour, to their applause.

Edgar had delegated all that in order to keep his hands free. He filmed the entire time so that Louis wouldn't miss a thing. I don't know how much my son picked up exactly, but I can say with certainty that my mother watched every moment of my performance.

Jesus, if she'd been there with me, I'd seriously have contemplated strangling her. She didn't stop cackling in my ears, and she'd rounded up half the hospital to watch. I do believe there was a peak audience of a dozen Parisian spectators, openly making fun of me. She explained to them – laughing her head off – that I'd always been absolutely hopeless at sport, that finding her middle-aged kitten had all these hidden talents was an amazing discovery, and that the yellow, green and pink streaks in my hair finally revealed my inner punk to one and all.

The torture lasted over three hours. I yelled at Edgar that it was freezing, I stopped, I set off again, I forced myself to smile when all those adorable Hungarians cheered me on, but I was on my knees.

'You didn't exactly run the Color wotsit half marathon, but you could say you *walked* it,' teased my mother in front of a gathering used to her wisecracks by now.

After two hours, I wasn't laughing any more. I sent the headphones flying. I was behaving like a woman in labour – insults and crushed hands included – but Edgar stayed calm throughout. Despite the pain and the superhuman effort this challenge demanded of me, I was touched that Edgar had gone to so much trouble.

The torment ended in front of the dome of Saint Stephen's Basilica, in the heart of Belváros, Pest's 'inner city'. I collapsed. Edgar gave me a piggyback to our little apartment, which was only a stone's throw from there. It had an incredible vintage bath that I'd been dreaming about all day. I lay soaking for a good hour, gently massaging my aching calves and thighs. When I got out, I flung myself on to my bed and didn't open my eyes until early the next morning.

*

Edgar and I spent the next day being tourists. I rediscovered the places I'd run through, and this time I was able to appreciate them properly: the steep streets on Castle Hill, the soaring Matthias Church spire, the majestic Parliament Building, the stately Danube – not exactly blue – and the trendy shops and restaurants in the Erzsébetváros district.

I loved Budapest as much as Tokyo. Two cities that could not be more different. But both of them had a touch of innocent madness that resonated with Louis's character.

I loved every nook of those cities as if they were pieces of my son.

*

Louis had perfectly summed up our evening activity in his notebook. We were to go in for a different type of competition. A 'party marathon', described as follows:

Have a drink in a dozen ruin bars and then stay out all night at the wild techno party in the Széchenyi Baths!!! (All without throwing up, please.)

I hoped that Louis had planned to wait until he reached the legal age before embarking on the alcohol-sodden adventures on which he was sending me, but I very much doubted it. When I was a teenager, I too would have a little drink, naively thinking I'd pulled the wool over my mother's eyes, until she told me one day, without batting an eyelid, that my breath stank and that I couldn't teach an old dog to drink beer.

The weather was freezing, but Edgar and I soon warmed up wandering from *kert* to *kert*. These 'ruin bars' are in abandoned courtyards in the old Jewish quarter. Disorientating places of decadent beauty, cleverly designed grunge decors, where Budapest's cosmopolitan youth chills out at night. We ate in one of them, to soak up the alcohol that had even seeped into our frozen toes, then, with a mix of apprehension and excitement, we headed for the rave at the Széchenyi Baths.

The place was crazy. Széchenyi, the most famous of Budapest's thermal baths, was a magnificent edifice that looked like a neo-baroque palace. We were outdoors, in sub-zero temperatures, and the spa waters were thirty-eight degrees Celsius. The ochre-coloured walls contrasted with the blue glow of the baths, and the dense steam rising from the swimming pools muted the whiteness of the snow-covered statues. In these funky surroundings, thousands of young people, completely sloshed, were dancing in swimsuits to hardcore techno, jumping up and down to the flashing lasers in a doomsday scenario.

I too started to move – I had no choice, otherwise I'd freeze to death. Timidly, at first. I watched Edgar out of the corner of my eye. The strobe made him look like a Roman statue. He turned towards me, smiled and leaned over to speak. He said, 'We're not going to stay like this, watching life pass us by.' Maybe I misunderstood. Maybe he didn't say that. Maybe I imagined it. Edgar took my hand and led me into the centre of the crowd.

We danced like kids, for hours and hours, until we were exhausted. Teenagers barely older than my son danced with me ... I laughed and tried to bounce around like them. Creased up with laughter, Edgar filmed it all.

We were far too old for all these experiences, but

letting our hair down like that felt so good. It was wonderful to forget about being reasonable for a short while. I realized that, once out of my twenties, I'd decided to start behaving like a responsible adult. I sneered at those thirty-somethings hanging out at rock concerts, those gamers devoting entire nights to their online heroes, those others whose free time was devoted to generating 'likes' on social networks. They were all adrenaline junkies, behaving as if they were still fifteen, still thrill-seeking, busting their guts in their futile pursuit of fun. Maybe, ultimately, they were right.

That night, my son helped me revive a few too-quickly-turned pages of my youth. That night, I understood that life – true life, which stays in your memory – is nothing other than a succession of moments of freedom. And that no adult ambition can make a person happier than the teenage ability to seize the moment.

We took a taxi back, picked up our luggage and went straight to the airport, still numb from the cold and dazed from the loud music.

Both of us exhausted, but happy.

Excerpt from the Book of Wonders

Push boundaries ☺

    – Take part in The Color Run and get to the end. The Budapest race sounds cool . . . especially because it turns into the party marathon I saw on MTV.

    – So, the party marathon: have a drink in a dozen ruin bars and then stay out all night at the wild techno party at the Széchenyi Baths. (All without throwing up, please.)

19

5 to 3 Days

TEAM SPIRIT

Over the past few days, we'd been a real team. At the hospital, the motley collection of individuals, aged from twelve to sixty, who were keeping watch on my son around the clock had been dubbed 'team Louis'. I always found it hard to admit publicly, but sharing the burden with team Louis did me the world of good.

For the following challenge – in Paris, this time – I decided to recruit Isadora. We had to fine-tune our act, because Louis's goal was far from easy. We rehearsed a little mother–daughter number that was totally insane. Ordinarily so poised, sensible and friendly, Isadora had to give a credible performance as a temperamental teen, swear like a trooper and vent her frustration with tears and tantrums. Truth be told, Isa was having the time of her life. Contrary to what she'd told me during our football training, she was not a terrible actress at all, and in fact played the part so well that she frightened her father. Isa flew into a rage when Edgar said he didn't have the two euros she wanted to buy her favourite magazine. She stamped her foot, flushed crimson and began to sob. I applauded her performance, she bowed and we burst out laughing at Edgar's half-astonished, half-relieved look. For a moment, he'd really believed that his daughter had completely lost it.

Having perfected our number, we put on our glad rags and headed for the N.R.J. Music Awards party, which was taking place that evening, 14 February, Valentine's Day. Once inside the building, we marched determinedly towards the stage door. As expected, it was guarded by two giant bouncers. Isadora was chewing gum outrageously, keeping her nose glued to her phone. She seemed to be developing a taste for her role. Edgar would have to watch out, in a few years' time . . .

The Hégémonie group was one of the event's sponsors. So I flashed my old business card, which said I was the company's marketing director. A card with a gilt logo, like that, intimidated people. I acted the stressed-out, borderline-hysterical executive, swearing I'd left my accreditation in the taxi, and I dropped a few names of senior people in the company – I'd done my homework thoroughly. I kept this act up for ten long minutes, and, faced with the bouncers' reasonable refusal to let me past, I produced my trump card: my daughter for the evening. Isadora began to yell, calling on the security guards as witnesses, telling them that not only did she never get to see me because of my job, but – worse – every time I promised her something, I screwed it up. That I'd promised to take her backstage, and a promise was a promise. In a final theatrical flourish, she sat down on the floor and sobbed her heart out. A young woman with a V.I.P. badge came over to us, said a few words to Isadora, then turned to the security guards and said, 'They're with me; let them through.' Bingo.

Once past, we thanked the pretty young woman, who gave Isa a kiss and asked if everything was OK now. She was sorry to leave us there, but she had to go and get ready. Isa threw her arms around my neck in a daze, thanking me a thousand times for allowing her to kiss Lulu something or other – her schoolfriends would be sooo jealous.

'I allowed you to kiss Lulu who?'

'Louane Emera. She's a really famous singer? OK, you've obviously never heard of her . . . I know, for the past two years, you've been shut away in your cave, listening to Wham! records, haven't you?'

I'd never seen Isa so bubbly. She didn't stop smiling all evening.

We wandered around backstage, then we froze. We were close to our goal. Holding our breath, we pushed open the door on which a clumsily Sellotaped plain sheet of A4 paper announced soberly, *Maître Gims*.

He was there, but he wasn't alone. He leapt up, two

men and a woman barred our path and tried to push us back. Isa managed to wriggle past and sum up the reasons for our intrusion in a few seconds: Louis, the coma, the notebook, our mission, his invaluable help. OK, our sheer gall, as well. I don't know whether he believed us, but the guy started to laugh and said, 'OK.'

'Super cool, super swag, a legend,' declared Isadora as we left some minutes later. She still couldn't get over it, but, in her phone, she had the irrefutable proof: I'd jammed with the rapper Maître Gims. I can tell you that hearing myself screech, *'Elle répondait au nom de Bella . . .'* was worth its weight in peanuts, as my mother would say.

*

The following morning, I took Isa with me into Louis's hospital room, for the first time. She hadn't seen him since the accident. Of course, I'd prepared her, explaining that he'd lost a lot of weight, that he was pale, his features were sharper, and he was hooked up to countless machines. I was used to seeing him like that, but the reality was hard for Isa's tender little heart to take. She cried silently for a while, watching Louis and holding his hand. She kissed him on the cheek. For me, too, that scene was gruelling. I managed to hide my emotion, but I couldn't help thinking that Louis might never know what it was to be in love. That he might never feel that glow in the pit of his stomach, desire, the need to feel his arms around another person.

Isa gradually regained her composure, her voice, her natural language, and told Louis about our evening, Louane's kiss, my a cappella with Maître Gims. I think she played him the soundtrack of my little private gig a dozen times. I didn't have such a bad voice, after all. 'Maybe you chose the wrong career,' teased Charlotte, who'd joined us.

That seemingly harmless joke deeply perturbed me. No, I had no ambition to become a singer, but, yes, I had chosen the wrong career. Or, rather, I'd chosen the wrong life.

I had no wish to carry on with my job from before. I had no wish to carry on with my life from before. In fulfilling my son's dreams at high speed, I'd blown apart my relationships with other people, and the very idea of my future.

Of my previous life, I only wanted to keep the foundations. Those pillars that stood firm, come rain or shine: my fragile structure. My mother. The upbringing she'd given me. My culture. My values. My memories.

And, above all else, my son.

Excerpt from the Book of Wonders

Push the boundaries!!!! (cont.)
– Meet Maître Gims or Black M . . . but, most importantly, do a duet with one of them!!!! (Otherwise it's too easy!)

It Hurts, But It Doesn't Matter

Today, Mum's voice sounded weird – sort of sad and happy at the same time. Her voice has been like that for several days. It's like it's changed. Before, her voice was just sad (except when she was telling me about the adventures from my notebook, then she was LOL (that means 'laughing out loud', for the over-forties)).

Since my ears are the only bit of me that works, I've become acutely sensitive to details, to changes in intonations. I'd never realized how much you could grasp just from listening. On the TV, there are programmes where they pretend to judge singers purely on their voices, but everyone knows that's crap, because, before they appear on stage, the competitors are preselected by people who've seen them. Result: not many ugly ones, just a few to make it look more authentic, but they're thrown out in the later stages, seeing as they're ugly. The ugly people always lose at some point – that's the rule. Me, if I was one of the judges, I'd make sure the ugly ones won, because now I know how important it is to really listen to people without being affected by appearances. If you listen closely to someone, if you concentrate hard, it's as if you

171

can see them. No, it's even better: you hear what the person says and also what they don't say. Me, I listen to the silences, the hesitations, the words they choose, the ones that slipped out and they wish they hadn't said, the melody, the humour, their breathing. That's all I do. I decipher, I understand voices.

I've picked up on several things in Mum's voice recently. Three, to be exact. Three things that Mum hasn't told me, but which I've sussed anyway.

The first one is that Mum's got a crush on Edgar. I'm convinced. That's new, too. I've never ever heard Mum talk about someone in such glowing language. I must admit, I'm super envious. She talks all the time about what she did with Edgar, or – worse – and this makes me a thousand times more envious – with Isa. Over the past few days, she's involved both of them in the challenges in my Book of Wonders. At first, it made me sick. I had the feeling that Edgar and Isa were taking my place in Mum's heart. Now, I'm still envious, I can't help it. But I really like Edgar and I adore Isa, so I tell myself that, if I am going to be replaced, it may as well be by the best league players. So, I listen to Mum telling me about my dreams and living my life in my stead with her new friends. It hurts not to be part of it all, but, at the same time, it does me no end of good! Mum's had so much fun turning the pages and doing the things written in my notebook. She always manages to make me laugh my head off and cheer me up when she tells me about her adventures. I'm sure it's good for me to be shaken up, even though I can't move.

She's wowed me again, several times.

When she ran her paint-splattered half marathon in Budapest and managed to get to the end, she blew me away. Mum had told me she wasn't sure she'd be able to run that distance, and that it was a good thing that Edgar was going with her to help, coach and support her, and bring her back if she passed out. I told myself she could have asked someone else, of course, but when I heard Charlotte and Grandma giggling the day before Mum and Edgar left for Hungary, I figured that something was going on. That really hurt. It made me feel that Mum had decided that life would go on for her, without me. Because, actually, I think Mum had a good time in Budapest. And Edgar supported her and protected her, she told me with a thing in her voice that sounded like hero worship. Yes, as I said, I'm envious.

A little while ago, Mum came into my room with Isa. At the time, I was thrilled that Isa had come to see me, even if I imagined that seeing me like this must be a real passion-killer. Yesterday, Mum went to the N.R.J. Music Awards party with Isa. She was determined to tick one of the boxes that I thought was the hardest, and she did it. She's crazy, my mother. I laughed, I cried, I thought it was genius that she did that duet with Maître Gims, because I know how much Mum hates rap, but, once again, I nearly died of jealousy that Isa went with her.

Of course, I want Mum to carry on living and to see people again. But, at the same time, I hate the idea because it means that I'm becoming less important. That soon I'll be part of the furniture, and the centre of Mum's world will be somewhere else, with Edgar, with Isa, with Grandma, with Charlotte. When Mum talks to Charlotte, she says 'tu' now, and it's obvious that they share a life outside the hospital, a life in which they see and talk to each other. I get the impression they've become mates. That's weird, because, from her voice, I get the sense that Charlotte's much younger than Mum. Everything's so strange and nothing's strange any more. When I think about it, I get the impression that Mum's got younger. Maybe that's what's really changed in her voice.

Mum's done almost everything I wrote in my notebook. She's nearly finished and I find that very frightening. What's going to happen next? I try not to think about it, but actually I think about it all the time, because the second thing that Mum hasn't said, but which I've clocked anyway, is that she's got new plans. She wants to start her life afresh, she's got ideas for a new job, too, I'm certain, and that drives me mad because I know that, for Mum, her work is all-important. With all these people and a new gig, where does that leave me? On the fourth floor of the Robert Debré Hospital. Not in her life any more.

The last thing that Mum isn't saying, the thing that's the most painful, is that any hope that I'll wake up is fading. I've concluded that they've given her a date. I don't know when it is, but I sense it's very close. I feel it when she tells me to keep fighting, that I can do it: she doesn't have the same strength as she did a few days ago. Sometimes she sounds resigned. At those times, I want to yell that I've been awake for donkey's *years (as Granny Odette would say), but that no one gives a stuff, that those stupid doctors aren't even capable of seeing it, despite their umpteen qualifications and their state-of-the-art equipment. A shit show, that's what this hospital is. Excuse my language, but I've had it up to here. What does Mum think? I feel that, if my body doesn't start sending signals, I'm going to give up soon. If I'm still hanging in here, it's purely for her sake! For everything she's done for me, for everything she's still doing, I'm only sticking around for her. Because, me, I'm beginning to accept the idea. I understand that I'm an immobile object, a burden that has no useful purpose. I'm not even decorative – decorative, what a joke! I know I've got tubes sticking out all over my body, that they stuff pre-chewed mush directly into my stomach, that they put me in nappies, like a baby or an old person. I picture myself, I see myself, and I'm disgusted. I must be horribly ugly, and, with no voice to wow the jury,* Hop it, out, sweep him away, bring on the next contestant. *Mum tells me I'm beautiful. I don't believe her, but it makes me happy to hear it anyway. Grandma tells me that I'm her miracle, that my room's ready at home, that there are loads of presents waiting for me.*

But I've started to tell myself that I'm certainly going to die. The first time I thought about it, it was super, super hard. I cried inside, a lot, for a long time. It was impossible to know how long, but it felt like ages. I've thought about it every day ever since, and now I'm resigned. Perhaps it won't be so bad for Mum and Grandma, after all. They come and see me in hospital every day – that's not a life. So I tell myself that, if I were dead, well, they'd be upset at first, but then it would pass and things would be better. Things always pass. Little Louis was cute, but it was better to put an end to it, because seeing him like that was slowly destroying his family. And I don't want to destroy Mum. I don't want to destroy Grandma. They don't deserve it. It would be better for them if I gave up. That's what I tell myself every day.

But I can't. I don't know why, but I can't accept that it's over. Deep down, something is telling me I can still wake up. Actually, it's not something saying that, it's someone. Mum. I want to see her again. Hug her tight. Even if it was just once, it would be worth the fight. I'd like to say thank you to her. Tell her I love her. Tell her that she's the best mother in the world. Just once. Well, if it's more than once, that'd be OK too ... Then I could die, if that's what's meant to be. I know I keep contradicting myself, but try to understand, imagine yourself in my place. What would you do? Give up or carry on? I simply listen. No choice; it's the only option available.

When I hear Mum, even with her new voice, she sounds as if she still wants me to wake up. So I've got to keep trying.

20

Day 3

LOUIS'S HERITAGE

I asked to see Dr Beaugrand at the end of the day. He had a solemn expression and seemed worn out, a distant look in his eye. For a moment, I thought he was trying to avoid me, but I was there and I was waiting for news.

Over the past few days, I'd sensed something was happening inside Louis, even though the electroencephalograms were still as haphazard. But I could see signs that the others didn't seem to have picked up. Or, at any rate, didn't interpret in the same way. For some time now, Louis's body had regularly trembled with slight spasms, movements. Reflexes – nothing conscious, nothing coordinated, nothing logical. I agreed with the diagnosis, how could I not? I was so desperate to see some meaning in the brief clenching of a hand, the twitch of a cheek or a foot, in those soft yelps. But they happened randomly, sometimes even while his brain was being scanned ... and the tests were still showing the same anarchic pattern. And yet, in the past few days, I'd noticed some changes. Real changes. The intensity when he clenched his hand was different at different times, I was certain of it. And, most importantly, I'd noticed that the movements were more frequent and lasted longer when I was speaking to him. As if he were trying to communicate. No one in this damned hospital would listen to me – or, rather, everyone listened to me, everyone knew the situation. The countdown. Hope does your head in, makes you imagine an awakening that isn't happening. So, when I spoke about Louis, people's faces changed. I could see the pity and what they were really thinking in their eyes: *She's losing her mind as well as losing her son, it's not surprising . . . It'll all be over soon, in any case.*

But I was certain of what I was seeing, of what I felt. Maternal instinct. I'd never really understood what that meant. Now, the expression really resonated and seemed so utterly appropriate. Maternal instinct means seeing things others can't see, feeling the slightest fluctuation in your child's behaviour in your bones. I could feel Louis. I could feel Louis, and Louis was talking to me.

That was why I wanted to speak to Dr Beaugrand. I thought he would listen to me, that he'd try to do something. He listened to me, his face blank. He had the direct look of the expert navigator whose job it was to bring those who are adrift back to the shore. Charlotte was with me. She spoke in my defence, arguing that I was the one who spent the most time with Louis, that, statistically, if anything happened, I was the one who had the greatest chance of witnessing it, so account should be taken of my observations and views.

Alexandre Beaugrand told me I should prepare myself for the worst, adding that the medical team was increasingly concerned because there was no change in Louis's condition and the clinical evidence was undeniable. To show his willingness, and because he accepted Charlotte's reasoning, he was prepared to increase the frequency of the electroencephalogram over the last remaining days, but he did not share my observations, or my conviction. *Over the last remaining days.* Alexandre Beaugrand had just stabbed me brutally in the back. I concluded that he couldn't be a father – which Charlotte confirmed. How would he handle these situations when he was able to apply feelings he had personally experienced to other people's tragedies? How would he react when the face of his own youngster superimposed itself on the ashen face of a child in the final stages of life?

Charlotte took me home. I didn't feel like seeing either Edgar or Isadora.

I knew there'd be something with Edgar, one day. It was a certainty I had a gut feeling about, which was reinforced by the time we spent together. But, right now, my heart was closed to everyone except my son. Edgar would have to be patient. He assured me he would be, and I wanted to believe him. At any rate, I didn't want to think about that sort of thing, not at present. So, I let things take their course, I let things go.

When we were on our way back from our trip to Budapest, in the taxi taking us to the airport, we exchanged a kiss. Or rather, our lips brushed. Chaste, pure. Let it stay that way for now.

'I can't give you any more,' I whispered.

'I don't expect any more,' he replied, taking my hand. 'We have plenty of time. Think about Louis, do what you have to do. Don't have any regrets.'

Three days to go until the end. I needed my mother by my side. To have her squeeze me. Hard. My mother and I had never been very demonstrative, but I do believe that, over the past few weeks, we'd made up for a good ten years or so. I couldn't get to sleep any more without her. Finding myself alone in my bedroom terrified me, I needed to feel her warm body next to mine, and I could tell she needed that too. Every day, my mother repeated the words she spoke too rarely when I was a child: I love you. My mother and I were experiencing a total revolution. Why had it taken such a tragedy for us to discover how much we meant to each other? Why had we ruined all those years hating each other through all that remained unspoken, when, deep down, nothing was broken? So much time lost, so many missed opportunities, so much emotional damage.

I needed my mother to face the challenge that Louis had set me for the next day. I'd turned the page in the Book of Wonders. It was the penultimate entry. After this, there'd be just one left, and then that would be the end. I wiped away the tears welling up in the corners of my eyes.

There was just one line. I'd dreaded that line. I'd wondered at what point it would appear, but I knew it would be there. Painfully logical.

– *Find out who my father is. And see him, just once.*

I'd had a relationship for nearly two years with Louis's father. It was a typical story, I realize with hindsight. At the time, I'd felt as if I was living in a fairy tale, a waking dream. That had made the fall hurt all the more.

I met Matthew in May, fifteen years ago. I was sitting at a pavement café on Place de la République. It was a very hot day, and Parisian women had finally ditched their woollen sweaters for the irresistible combo of sunglasses and strappy tops, while the tourists displayed their sweaty armpits. Matthew was sitting at the next table, with the Lonely Planet guide to Paris in one hand, and a beer in the other. No perspiration rings – that was a point in his favour. I noticed him at once. Matthew exuded sexiness: tall, greying at the temples, athletic looking. He reminded me a little of George Clooney in *Ocean's Eleven*. Branded shades, a white shirt with the sleeves rolled up – very important, long sleeves on a shirt; for me, that shows good taste. Slow gestures, even when he picked up his beer, delicate fingers – not the sort to get his hands dirty. An intellectual. Forty-something. I had just turned twenty-four. He could have been my father. That was probably one of the main things that attracted me, because I'd never had a father. I only admit this subconscious Oedipal pull with hindsight. At the time, I don't think I was aware of it.

I was reading an excruciatingly boring management book, and my gaze was naturally drawn to the neighbouring table. After a few moments, I could feel his eyes on me. He smiled and I noticed the dimple that appeared on his right cheek. Louis has one in the same place – totally adorable. He asked me if I could help him; he was on his own in Paris and was looking for a good restaurant for that evening. He lived in London, was on a work trip. Two whole weeks. So, rather than going backwards and forwards, he'd chosen to spend the weekend in France. He didn't regret staying. I laughed, and he added, with a mischievous twinkle in his eye, that he was talking about the lovely weather compared to rainy London, of course. Of course.

Matthew had an art gallery in Notting Hill. He spoke French with a charming accent, and had a slightly caustic sense of humour. So British. How could a man like that still be single? He hadn't found his princess, that was all, but he hadn't given up hope. Paris was the capital of love, wasn't it? Matthew wanted to go up the Eiffel Tower, at night. See the city at his feet. He asked me to go with him. I warned him that there'd be long queues, that we'd have to wait ages. Matthew was better informed than I was. At the last minute, he managed to book a table at the fine-dining restaurant at the top of Paris's emblematic monument, which allowed us to jump the queue of tourists. A very expensive privilege, but so romantic.

I fell in love with Matthew that first evening. I'd just started working at Hégémonie. My first job. I gave myself, one hundred per cent, to my employer, not knowing that fifteen years later it would still be the same. Matthew and I had a passionate long-distance love affair. Twenty-three months, to be exact. We met once a fortnight. Two entire weekends each month – usually, one in Paris, the other in London. Matthew actually visited Paris regularly, and knew the city inside out. I learned much later that the Lonely Planet on his table was part of his baiting strategy. That I wasn't the first Parisienne to fall into his trap.

In Paris, he usually came to my place, but sometimes he preferred to go to a luxury hotel, and we'd spend the entire weekend between the bed, the private pool and the restaurant. When he was in Paris with me, he was with me. 'A matter of principle, *beautiful*.' Matthew called me *beautiful*. I'd never felt as beautiful as when I was in his arms. Nothing was too good for his princess. I was his spoilt baby. We spent our time blissfully locked away together.

In London, I wanted to meet his friends. He told me he wanted me all to himself, only for him. He'd meet me on the Friday evening, at the gallery, when everyone had left. Sex with Matthew was impatient, urgent, sometimes on the floor, surrounded by the artworks, my weekend bag flung in a corner. Sex with Matthew was passionate, with no half measures, with biting, groans of pleasure and post-coital bliss. Sex with Matthew was intoxicating, I developed a taste for the glass of champagne we drank naked after orgasming, savouring the earthquake amid the priceless contemporary debris. I'd never felt that way about anyone before. He'd never felt that way about anyone before. He did his utmost to preserve the extraordinary nature of our affair. Sometimes, we went to what he called his 'little pad', a tiny apartment in Notting Hill that was nothing special, around the corner from the gallery. But, in London, as in Paris, Matthew liked to take me to incredible hotels, fabulous settings for our love – that was the exact expression he used. Better still, I sometimes had the surprise of finding in my letterbox a proper handwritten invitation, with a plane ticket to Barcelona, Dublin, Venice or Lisbon. The old-fashioned charm of pure, simple romanticism. Of the successful – not to mention rich – man who showers his soulmate with kindness. I kept telling him it was madness. He invariably replied that money was for making the people you loved happy – otherwise, what was the point of it?

I wanted to believe that this was life with Matthew.

In reality, it was everything but life.

In the twenty-third month of our relationship, I became pregnant. It wasn't planned. I went to see my doctor, describing my symptoms. I felt tired all the time, I vomited sometimes, my energy level dropped in the middle of the day. Had I been having periods? My periods were irregular, I hadn't had one for a while, but that wasn't unusual. I didn't see the connection. It hadn't even occurred to me. When the pregnancy test showed two blue lines, I cried my eyes out. I didn't want this child, not now, not like this. My life was all mapped out. I was planning to have a child when I was around thirty, not before. Before was too soon. My career at Hégémonie was my priority, and Matthew and I still had so much more we wanted to do. Matthew didn't want children, he'd been very clear about that. I'd always told myself I'd manage to convince him, when the time was ripe. Certainly not now.

But, gradually, the tiny bird unfurling its wings in

my belly started to carve out a place for itself. At first, discreetly, then more and more insistently. I caught myself in the middle of a meeting, imagining the child I might have. I didn't say anything to Matthew, and I didn't see him for a whole month. I wanted to make the decision on my own, and I also wanted to avoid him discovering the truth. Five weeks later, my mind was made up. The feeling was visceral. I was going to keep the baby. It would be a girl and I'd call her Louise. Matthew would be besotted with us. I'd move to London. We'd be happy.

I prepared a charade in two languages to inform Matthew of the good news. He'd be shocked, of course, but I was certain he'd be over the moon, after the initial surprise. I took the Eurostar and went straight to the gallery, in the middle of the day, a Thursday. It was the first time I'd gone to meet Matthew without warning. He so loved giving me surprises, but this time he'd be on the receiving end for once!

A woman in her forties opened the door at the gallery. Elegant, sophisticated, in a Chanel suit. Frosty. A businesslike smile, looking me up and down scornfully as her eye roved over my H&M clothes and my Bata shoes. I asked to see Matthew, but he wasn't there. Who wanted to know? Thelma – a friend.

'I see . . .' the woman replied.

What did she see, exactly?

'Matthew has many women friends, you know, he's a very busy man . . .'

I didn't like this woman's insinuations about Matthew at all, and, anyway, who was she? As far as I knew, he'd always run the gallery on his own, like the big man he thought he was. She held out her hand and introduced herself, in an English that was both impeccably polite and condescending.

'Delighted to meet you, Thelma. I'm Deborah. I help my husband out by looking after the gallery when he's away. Matthew travels a lot. He's very fond of Paris and Parisian women. I'm not jealous, I assure you. The agreement we made many years ago allows me to live my life as I please, too. But, I must say, Matthew usually has better taste in women. You really are nothing special. Good day, mademoiselle.'

I never saw Matthew again. I never contacted him again.

He never knew I was pregnant. He'd never seen Louis.

He tried to call several times over the weeks following my encounter with his wife. I didn't respond. He kept trying. One day, I sent him a text: *Deborah is very beautiful. You're a stupid bastard. Don't ever try to contact me again.*

I was three months pregnant.

Nearly thirteen years later, I switched on my computer and did a search for his name. I'd never done that,

187

despite the ease with which the god Google spat out information to anyone who asked. I had forbidden myself to do so; that book must stay closed. It didn't take long for my search to produce results. Matthew still ran the same gallery, at the same address. How old was he now? Fifty-seven, fifty-eight? I clicked on the *Images* thumbnail and received a shock. Louis was the spitting image of Matthew, the resemblance was striking. I stared wide-eyed at the photos of recent exhibition openings. Matthew, glass of champagne in hand, broad smile. Matthew, arms folded, tight-fitting suit and salt-and-pepper hair, posing in front of the works of an obscure New York artist. Matthew, still as good-looking. How many other Thelmas had he ensnared? I scrolled down the page. Then I saw her – sure of herself, of her power. Whatever Matthew had got up to, she was still there. Deborah was smiling, Matthew's arm around her waist.

I suddenly wanted to throw up.

I was thirteen years pregnant. I was going to have to deal with my nausea.

The address was 80 Portobello Road. I could have found my way there blindfolded.

21

Day 2

REMINDERS

I took an early-morning Eurostar. The Gare du Nord was heaving. I found myself caught up in a school party on its way to London – the kids probably around Louis's age. My initial reflex was that of the uptight middle-class woman. I sought out the train manager, determined to try to move to a different carriage. And then I had a change of heart. I sat down in my seat. I was at a table with three year-eight kids – class 8D, from the Collège Anatole France in La Roche-sur-Yon. I talked football and Pokémon cards with them, and they were gobsmacked that I was capable of having such a conversation. I showed them the video of me jamming with Maître Gims and earned their lifelong respect. They asked for my autograph. I'd touched their idol, which, by association, made my signature priceless. I didn't notice the time going past. I'd stopped navel-gazing and it was doing me good.

On arrival at St Pancras, I took a taxi to Notting Hill. I didn't give the exact address. I needed to walk for a few minutes, to decompress. I didn't want to turn up right outside Matthew's gallery; I wanted to watch it first from the outside, before going in. I couldn't have coped with another encounter with Deborah. The last one was thirteen years ago, but I was still smarting from it.

I stationed myself on the pavement opposite. I'd put on sunglasses and had taken care with my hair and clothes to create a radically different look from the one that Matthew knew. Until the last minute, I wanted to be able to choose whether to go in or not. I didn't want to risk him taking the initiative, or for him to see me before I'd decided I wanted him to.

He was there. Alone. Poring over his smartphone. I thought he looked old. He had aged more than his online photos had showed, the previous day. I breathed in and breathed out. Three times. Then three more times. I crossed the street and pushed open the door, and an ancient little bell rang. Matthew looked up at me. He blanched. He'd recognized me at once. He muttered my name, and simply said, 'What are you doing here?' Then he smiled. I was flung back fifteen years. No, he wasn't so old. He was still very attractive. I looked down for a moment and asked myself whether Louis had been conceived on that cold floor. Memories came flooding back. Bitter. Beautiful. And terribly vivid.

My mobile vibrated. I ignored it. Not now. I'm busy. I have to tell the father of my child that he has a twelve-year-old son. A superb adolescent who's the spitting image of him. And he is in a coma. Two days away from a potentially tragic sentence.

I hesitated. Cold sweat ran down my back; I started breathing faster. I suddenly became aware of the cruel absurdity of the situation. What kind of woman was I, for heaven's sake? Could I really spill out the whole unfiltered story, now? Despite all the hurt Matthew had caused me, could I announce these two things, one on top of the other, after thirteen long years? What did I know of his life now? How would he take it? Maybe he had a heart condition, maybe I'd kill him if I threw all this in his face. Would I be able to look my son in the eyes afterwards?

I leaned against the handle of the glass door. Louis wanted to see his father, just once. I'd seen him. My mission was accomplished. I went hot and cold, I felt my knees about to give way, but they held out. I said nothing. I backed out of the door. Matthew took a few steps forward. I retreated further. My feet reached the pavement of Portobello Road. I ran. A light drizzle misted my face and the sunglasses I was still wearing. Matthew came out into the street and called after me several times. He tried to catch up with me, but I knew he couldn't leave the gallery unattended and would soon abandon the chase.

My mobile vibrated again. Not now; I'm busy running away from my life, once again.

Eventually, I got on to a bus and allowed myself to be ferried away. Tears ran down my face. The rain beat against the window of the bus, the top deck of which was strangely empty.

I let my phone vibrate, and vibrate again.

The more it vibrated, the more certain I was.

No one had tried to contact me with such urgency for ages. There was only one possibility, one reason why anyone would be so desperate to contact me.

I listened to the last message. It was my mother. She asked me not to listen to the earlier messages and to meet her at the hospital as soon as I could. Her voice was trembling. She'd been crying. There were four earlier messages: three from my mother, and another from a number I knew only too well – the intensive-care unit at the Robert Debré Hospital.

I followed my mother's advice. I switched off my phone and put it away.

I took Louis's notebook out of my bag and caressed it. Pressed it to my shattered heart. I turned the pages, one at a time, slowly. Until I reached the last one. I read what my son was asking me to do. The rain was bucketing down, now. I couldn't hold back the words that formed unaided in my mind. The last page. His last wishes.

I stood up. I gave my telephone to a young woman sitting near me. Slightly confused, she thanked me.

Then I got off the bus.

22

Day 1

AVOIDANCE

I didn't call my mother back. I didn't call the hospital back.

As long as I hadn't been given the grim official news, Louis was alive. I decided to do the thing I knew how to do best: avoid.

I could see now with painful clarity how I've always been the queen of avoidance. When a situation gets tricky, my natural instinct is to run away. It was my spontaneous reaction. My way of protecting myself from gusts of wind, typhoons and cyclones. The stronger the wind, the stronger my urge to retreat. I need to build myself a temporary shelter to help me weather it. I'm not able to put out to sea in a storm. The swell has to subside a little. I've always been panic stricken at the thought of letting others read my feelings, especially when I'm not in control of them. That's when I resorted to avoidance. I avoided Matthew thirteen years ago, via a simple text message. I avoided Matthew a few hours ago, rather than allow myself to be overwhelmed. I avoided my mother, all those years. I've avoided my life and, in fulfilling Louis's dreams, I'd avoided my own.

Within hours of the end of the countdown, I'd avoided my son's death by inventing a future.

Avoidance is so much better than the truth.

I wanted to celebrate those last moments of sublime ignorance, allow myself a beautiful, pure night of hope. I wanted to be in a new and very special place. I'd read that there was a hotel in the avant-garde London skyscraper, the Shard. The major milestones in my life had always been celebrated with spectacular views. The Eiffel Tower, when I first met Matthew. The incredible hotel in Tokyo, to launch my son's Book of Wonders adventure. A high-rise in the shape of a majestic shard would be the perfect conclusion. I treated myself to a royal suite. I put London at my feet.

I ordered a bottle of French wine, from Provence, where my family's story had begun. Then I sat down at the desk of my unbelievable suite, and set about my unbelievable challenge. The last instructions that Louis had scribbled in his Book of Wonders were as simple to formulate as they were painful and complicated to execute. Especially at this point in my life. Especially at this moment in his life. It took me the entire night.

I avoided my son's death by gazing at the lights. I laid out my future life on blank sheets of a luxury London hotel's headed notepaper, and I included Louis in it. Furiously, frantically. One last time.

I remembered good things. I invented joys to come. I leapt into the unknown without a safety net. I laughed, I cried. I asked myself what woman I wanted to be. What I wanted to become – me, Thelma. What footprint I wanted to leave on this planet. I listened to myself. I asked myself what would make me happy. Truly happy. Forgetting everything that had governed my choices until now. Forgetting what society might expect of me. Forgetting what others might expect of me. I visualized it. I wrote it down. I stripped naked and faced myself. For the first time in my entire life. That night, I wrote my Book of Wonders. In the form dictated by Louis: a letter. I projected myself into a fantasy future. Which would probably never exist. Which might exist. It was a night of rare intensity.

At dawn, I looked up. I collected myself.

I avoid, but I always come back. When I've regained sufficient strength and courage, I pull myself together and confront. I bite, I fight.

I showered, put on my clothes from the previous day and clambered into a taxi to St Pancras. It was time for me to brave the storm.

Before boarding the train, I bought a disposable camera – the kind that was so common twenty years ago, but is now a vintage item. I took out of my purse the photograph that I always keep with me. In this faded snapshot, Louis is two years old. His face is smeared with chocolate and he's roaring with laughter. It's my favourite photo of my son. I held the camera up to the sky, placed the photo of Louis against my cheek, smiled and took a selfie.

The first of a series of 3,650 photos. An excellent idea to begin a last day, my son.

Excerpt from the Book of Wonders

In ten years . . .

*   – Write a letter to the person I'll be in ten years' time, imagining what my life will be like . . . to be opened and reread in ten years to the day – for a laugh.*

*   – Take a photo of myself every day to make a photomontage of my development: ten years in one minute.*

23

THE DAY WHEN . . .

I went straight to the hospital, without letting anyone know I was coming. It would take me twenty minutes or so from the Gare du Nord.

On the way, I hugged tight the envelope containing my writings and Louis's Book of Wonders. I had hot flushes. I was completely stressed out.

I'd had bouts of optimism during that London night. What if I'd misinterpreted my mother's message, her grave tone and quavering voice? Could she have been crying for joy? Yes, of course she could. But then why not just say in her message that Louis had woken up? When you've got good news, you don't beat about the bush. You leave an unambiguous message.

Yes, but she'd left three previous messages, which I hadn't listened to.

Yes, but the hospital had called too, and my mother had ordered me not to listen to the messages.

Yes, but . . . Yes, but . . . Hope. Damned hope. Which

never leaves its prey. I had been its willing victim for many long weeks.

I turned into the hospital's gloomy fourth-floor corridor. The nurses greeted me. I hastened my step. Now I was there, I had to see my son right away.

A nurse intercepted me and barred my path, saying, 'Wait a moment before you go in, please. Did you speak with Dr Beaugrand on the phone?'

She was blocking my access to the rest of the corridor. I looked at her, flabbergasted. I said no, I hadn't spoken with Dr Beaugrand, and that of course I was going to go into Louis's room, straight away. Charlotte came running up and grabbed my arm.

'Thelma, wait. I have to speak to you first.'

I was gripped by a feeling of sheer dread. I had to know. Now. I freed my arm and ran to Louis's room.

I opened the door.

I raced over to the bed.

Then, I saw.

24

HIS EYES

I saw his eyes.

They were open.

I began to cry.

I threw myself on to him. I hugged him and hugged him.

At first, he didn't respond.

Then he raised his right hand towards me and tried to articulate something.

I began to laugh manically, with that nervous laughter of someone who's cracking up. Someone whose nerves have suddenly given way. Someone whose dam has burst. My eyes were so full of tears that I could barely see him. I think the emotion I felt at that moment was as powerful as at his birth. No – even stronger. I was witnessing the second birth of my own child. His eyes were open, he was moving his hand, his arm, he was trying to speak. He was alive. Louis was alive. He'd done it. I'd done it, we'd done it. We were going to be able to carry on, together. Be happy, together. Always.

It was the most beautiful day of my life, I believe. It may sound stupid, said like that, but it was so true. What a beautiful day it was. How beautiful he was. How proud I was of Louis. Louis tried to speak, but I couldn't understand him. It would come. We had our whole lives for that. I talked to him, too. If there's one thing I've learned, it's that you should say what you feel. Always.

'My darling. I'm so happy. I'm here. I'm listening to you. You're amazing. You're so beautiful, my Louis . . .'

I moved away slightly to look at him.

I waited a little, and his face froze.

Then I saw.

His eyes.

I took a step back.

There was terror in his eyes.

My son tried to speak again.

And this time I understood. I understood what he was trying to say.

I understood the despair in that dark look.

I understood what Charlotte had meant, why she was in a hurry to talk to me *before* I went into that room.

My son, my love, my king.

Louis had just managed to utter, with great difficulty, three little words that pierced my heart:

'Who . . . are . . . you?'

25

ALIVE

I turned around. Mum came over and hugged me. She was crying. She kept saying that Louis was alive.

'He's alive. You've done it. It's thanks to you that he's come back, you can be certain of it. He'll remember. You wouldn't let us explain to you beforehand, you're so stubborn. The apple doesn't fall far from the tree . . . I also came rushing into the room, last night, and got into big trouble with the entire staff. We have to take it slowly, but his memory will come back.'

I was completely at a loss. Why had she left me a message telling me not to listen to the earlier messages?

'Because you had to come here, pussycat. Everyone had been trying to get hold of you for hours to tell you the news . . . There's a point where you have to say, "Enough, stop beating about the bush and act," and how could I have known that you'd follow any of my advice, when you always do exactly as you please? I'm sorry I made a shambles of things, as always . . .'

I looked at her and smiled. Only my mother would

talk about making a shambles of things at such a time. I looked up and met Charlotte's eyes. I asked her if what my mother had just told me was true, and that Louis would get his memory back.

'Oh, ye of little faith . . .' Mum retorted, which made us all laugh.

My mother has always been able to defuse the most serious situations – it's a real gift of hers. I would so like to have that ability, too.

Charlotte spoke softly. She gave me a hug as well. She smelled nice. I asked the question I'd been burning to ask: would Louis remember . . . me?

She answered that I'd have to speak to Dr Beaugrand, that he'd explain everything. That it was impossible to know whether Louis would get his memory back and, if so, what and who he would remember. Recovery after a coma varied from one person to another. What we were seeing was exceptional. Before opening his eyes, Louis had given no visible clinical signs of being awake. It had been sudden. And already, within a few hours, his progress had been swift. It would take a while to establish precisely which of his bodily functions were back to normal. Medicine had its limitations, and it was very hard to forecast. But we had to remain hopeful. My mother was right to be optimistic. It was obvious that his brain was working. He was trying to speak. He was moving his limbs. These were giant steps.

Charlotte also told me that I could be proud of what I'd done for him. What's more, a number of parents of other children in the hospital had begun to do likewise. I told her to stop kidding me, but she meant it. Even without a Book of Wonders, some parents had started asking their children what their most cherished dreams were, and fulfilling them. The children often had straightforward wishes that weren't so difficult to achieve. The joy of these new questions and rewards was spreading through the entire hospital. Of course, not all of these adventures would have a happy ending, but they were morale boosters. They injected doses of happiness, hope and life into existences devoted to fighting terrible diseases.

'You've done them an incredible amount of good, Thelma,' Charlotte went on. 'You're a role model for them.'

'Me? A role model? That's a first—'

'Don't do yourself down, darling,' my mother broke in. 'Be positive, for heaven's sake! You've done something extraordinary for your little boy, you're an inspiration to other parents – accept it, without tying yourself in knots. Celebrate, appreciate this enormous step you've helped Louis make. I know, before, you didn't know how to take your time, to relish things. But that was before. He's alive, for goodness' sake! Alive. We're all alive, and we're together.'

My mother was right. As always. Her words resonated with others – the ones I'd set down on paper, the previous night.

She was spot on.

I gazed around that room of wonders, which I would never forget. That emotional roller-coaster room, which had in turn broken me, shattered me, shaken me up, thrilled me, transcended and transformed me. That room, every square inch of which would remain etched in my mind.

My eyes roved over the walls, rested on a photo of me in shorts and football boots, between Isa and Edgar. I knew they were probably not far away, that they'd be here soon. All this kindness, all these people who cared about me – it was all new. In the course of this journey, I'd rediscovered the importance of those around me, those I'd call my close family and friends, and who, too often and too quickly, I'd distanced myself from. Might they be feeling the same way as me, right now? It was strange to feel a tiny flash of happiness in that cold, impersonal room.

I started to cry again.

For joy, and from giddiness at the thought of the unknown that lay ahead. But mostly for joy. Louis was alive. He really was.

I went over to him. I stroked his cheek and whispered to him not to be afraid, saying that I was his mum, and always would be, whatever happened. That I loved him, we loved him. That it was natural he couldn't remember anything right now, but I didn't hold it against him. I'd never hold anything against him. That I was so happy.

That tomorrow would be a new adventure. Each day would bring new surprises and discoveries. It would be a fresh opportunity for all of us, a new start, the possibility to reinvent ourselves and build something even more solid.

That he had to carry on fighting. It would be a long road, but he could lean on me. Lean on all of us. That I'd be there to support him, day and night. Come what may.

That there would be laughter. Love. Tears. Shouts. Football. Karaoke. Crazy parties, half marathons and car chases.

Joy, more of it. Happiness, always.

That he would remember.

And that, if he didn't remember the past . . . Well, we'd create new memories – simple.

I thought I could hear my mother.

I had heard a mother. It was me.

'I love you, Louis.'

He looked at me.

I think he smiled.

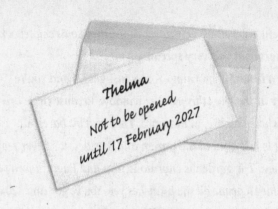

Thelma

Not to be opened until 17 February 2027

Thelma

Not to be opened until 17 February 2027

Dear Thelma,

When you read this letter, you'll be ten years older than you are at the time of writing. You're nearly fifty. You're still alive, despite all your overindulging – congratulations, that's no mean feat . . .

It's a beautiful morning. The sort of winter sky you so love. Winter 2017 is now just a dream. When you talk about that difficult time, you and Louis even manage to laugh about it. You haven't forgotten, of course. The memories are intact. Vivid. Time has polished them, your mind has gradually erased the pain, the contours are less sharp, beauty has taken its place. Louis often watches the videos you made with your mother. He always laughs when he watches you sing Johnny Hallyday in Tokyo. And, best of all, those images are now mixed in with others – the ones you took afterwards, when you went on exciting new adventures from Louis's notebook together. That was very special.

It's a beautiful morning. You've just got up and you're looking at the trees through the window. Because there are trees where you live, in Provence. They're a bit bare, but spring is just around the corner, and, besides, it's never really cold here. The garden is enormous. You and Edgar haven't had time to prune all the branches yet. You've got time. You've got all the time in the world. Edgar's already up, you can see him in the distance. He likes to rise very early, much earlier than you. It's his favourite time of day. He goes and sits by the lake below the house, alone, and he paints. You love watching him draw, paint, sculpt. Sometimes, you sit for him. Edgar is so talented.

It's a beautiful morning. You go downstairs into the big living room. Mum's already there, bustling about, getting breakfast ready. She smiles at you, asks if you slept well, calls you her pussycat, as always. You smile at her, kiss and hug her. It's your new morning ritual. You've become the most demonstrative mother–daughter duo in the world. Who would have believed it? You tell her you're going to help her, that there will be a lot of people this morning, that it's all hands on deck. She laughs and answers that she didn't wait for you to get started. You roll up your sleeves and start to lay the long, solid-wood table.

It's a beautiful morning. Yesterday, you had an email from Louis; he'll be there in a few hours. Louis is studying medicine. His stay in hospital triggered something in him. He's found his vocation. Not via a conventional route, admittedly. You would have preferred a session with a careers adviser to several weeks in a coma. But this is the result: Louis has decided he wants to be a paediatrician. At the moment, he's doing an internship at Great Ormond Street Hospital, in London. He's staying with Matthew for a few months. When those two met, it was a foregone conclusion. Matthew was annoyed with you for having kept Louis's existence from him. Then his anger gave way to the joy of discovering this surprise child.

It's a beautiful morning. Yesterday, Louis met up with Isadora at their place in Paris. They'll come down together on the train. When they're here, everyone thinks they're your children, that they're brother and sister. They're not wrong. They are your children. And when they kiss and there's an awkward silence, you burst out laughing and explain the situation. You're not an ordinary family. You never have been and never will be. Luckily. Isadora still plays football with Louis from time to time, but, nine years ago, she took up ballet again. And, today, her profession is the one her mother and grandmother dreamt of for her. She's following the path that's in her D.N.A. Isa and Louis are radiant, and it is a pure delight to watch them. You are so proud of the adults they are becoming.

It's a beautiful morning. In half an hour, the big living room will be filled with some twenty people. It's eight years, now, since you bought this big Provençal farmhouse, which you and Edgar fell in love with, using the compensation you were awarded after your legal battle against Hégémonie. It's a huge property, which you did up and converted into the most amazing place. This is where you decided to carry out the plan that had formed in your mind when Louis was in a coma. This is where you moved to, seven years ago, with Louis, Edgar, Isa and your mother. This is where Charlotte joined you all, a year later. She's part of the project, too.

It's a beautiful morning. You recall the day when you outlined your idea to your whole little gang. They were immediately up for it. They trusted you at once. They trusted the businesswoman you are. They trusted the mother you are. They trusted your intuition. Investors bought into it; they also believed in you.

It's a beautiful morning. The sun is already high in the sky, the table's ready. Your first guests are beginning to come downstairs. There's little Mathis, with his parents. They arrived the previous day. Mathis doesn't have any hair at the moment. It will grow back very quickly. In the meantime, he likes to dress up. You greet him Avengers-style, entering into his superhero game. He laughs and his smile brightens the start of your day. There's also Alice, who's been here for a week with her mother. Alice is already better. She's champing at the bit because, in an hour's time, she'll be meeting Edgar at the foot of the big olive tree for a sculpture session. She adores Edgar. Everyone adores him. Whether he's teaching them to draw or doing physical exercise, Edgar is universally loved.

And then there's your favourite, little Francesco. Francesco has been with you for nearly three weeks. His parents take it in turns to be with him, because they're divorced. This week, his father's here. Francesco's a comedian, who lights up the room. He and your mother form an unstoppable double act. In an hour, Odette and Francesco will do some gardening together, and then cook. Shrove Tuesday's already past, but they're planning to make pancakes, and your mother promised him he could toss them. Francesco is all excited.

It's a beautiful morning. The farmhouse is full. Your life is full. Most of the time you're here, in what is now your element. Sometimes you travel, because you're invited to speak to local authorities and entrepreneurs in France and abroad. They want to know how you designed and built all this. When you're away, Charlotte takes the reins. Charlotte has proved to be an excellent manager, in addition to having great nursing skills, which are always very useful here.

It's a beautiful morning. You walk down the little dirt track to pick up the post. On the letterbox is the name of your little paradise: The Rooms of Wonders.

It's a beautiful morning. You stroll back up to the house, taking the time to breathe in the Provençal country air, squinting because the sunlight is dazzling and memories come flooding back. It's like this every morning. The minute you see those words in purple lettering – a colour chosen by Louis – you recall the place where it all began. The room of wonders, room 405 in the Robert Debré Hospital, which gave you the

213

idea for this house. There, you realized the importance of family, of shared projects, for all those children and their loved ones. You understood that, for all those kids, the path back to life was long. That hospital could distance patients from their loved ones rather than bring them closer, whereas experiencing joyful things could be simple. That's why you decided to open this rather special holiday home. A house where children who've just come out of hospital – or who are given permission to have a few days away – come with their parents and their families. A house where everything is done to make them feel at home. Where you feel good. You have found your place. Useful. At last.

It's a beautiful morning. You glance at your watch. The same watch that was smashed when Louis had his accident. It, too, has been repaired. It, too, is a survivor. The time is 9:40. You walk faster, because soon your son's train will arrive. Soon, you'll be hugging him. You will tell him you love him, as always. Louis texted you yesterday to tell you the train time. The coincidence is disturbing, but it makes you smile. Louis is due on the 10:32.

It's a beautiful morning, Thelma. Make the most of your life. Make the most of those you love. You have all the time in the world. Take it.

Thelma,

London,

17 February 2017.

214

ACKNOWLEDGEMENTS

A huge thank you to my editor, Caroline Lépée. Thank you for your enthusiasm and your expertise. Thank you for believing in this book from the start.

Thank you to Philippe Robinet and the entire Calmann-Lévy team. It is a privilege to work with you. And a special thank you to Patricia Roussel and Julia Balcells; the *Kawaii Cat* landed on Saturn, thanks to you.

Thank you to Caroline R. for her advice. Thank you to Florence B. and Renaud M. for the memorable (and inspiring) trips to Tokyo.

Thank you to my family for their unflagging support and encouragement. To Alexandre and Andréa, my indispensable 'little bros'. To Floriane, Jules and Fanny, my avid readers. To my amazing parents-in-law, André and Raphaèle. To Pierre and Steph. To my grandfather, Pascal: keep telling me stories, it is precious. To Sandra, Jeanine and Aimé for the beautiful yesterdays.

To my mother and my father, of course. Mum, Dad, thank you for everything, and for always.

Thank you to my three loves. Alessandro and Éléonore, I am so proud of you ... my two wonders. Mathilde, none of this would mean anything without you at my side. To life, to life.